**"I have just one condition for accepting your job offer,"
Susannah said.**

David wheeled around, frustrated by the way she challenged him. "Which is?"

"When you disagree with my suggestions for your sister, and you will disagree," she said, her smile kicking up the corners of her pretty lips, "will you at least try to understand that I'm making my suggestions for Darla's benefit?"

What did she think—that he was some angry powermonger who had to lord it over everyone? "I'll listen," David agreed. "As long as you don't take any undue chances."

"With the baby?" Her face tightened. "I won't take any chances," she said firmly. "I want my baby to be healthy. I won't risk anything for that. That's the one decision I don't intend to mess up."

"Then we have a deal." David walked away, but his brain puzzled over her last comment. What did she mean?

He found no satisfactory answers to stop his thoughts about Darla's newest caregiver—at least, that was how he should be thinking of the beautiful Susannah Wells.

Easier said than done.

Books by Lois Richer

Love Inspired

Love Inspired Suspense

LOIS RICHER

likes variety. From her time in human resources management to entrepreneurship, life has held plenty of surprises. She says, "Having given up on fairy tales, I was happily involved in building a restaurant when a handsome prince walked into my life and upset all my career plans with a wedding ring. Motherhood quickly followed. I guess the seeds of my storytelling took root because of two small boys who kept demanding, 'Then what, Mom?'" The miracle of God's love for His children, the blessing of true love, the joy of sharing Him with others—that is a story that can be told a thousand ways and yet still be brand-new. Lois Richer intends to go right on telling it.

A Baby by Easter

Lois Richer

Love Inspired

LOVE INSPIRED BOOKS

Recycling programs
for this product may
not exist in your area.

ISBN-13: 978-0-373-87664-8

A BABY BY EASTER

www.LoveInspiredBooks.com

Printed in U.S.A.

It's in Christ that we find out who we are and what we are living for. Long before we first heard of Christ and got our hopes up, he had his eye on us for glorious living, part of the overall purpose he is working out in everything and everyone.

—*Ephesians* 1:11, 12
The Message

This story is for those generous souls
who open homes and hearts to kids of all ages
who crave love and affection. Your dedication
will be revealed in tomorrow's generation.

Chapter One

Evenings in Tucson were a lot cooler than the Los Angeles' dusk Susannah Wells was used to.

Remember, Suze, we foster kids never know about tomorrow. Save whatever you can so you'll be prepared.

Susannah squeezed her hand in her pocket, fingering the last bits of change leftover from her meager savings. Connie's advice about money had been right on, like so much other guidance she'd given in those long-ago days when they'd shared a room in their North Dakota foster home.

What advice would Connie have for her this time— or would she even want to be bothered with her former foster sister?

Susannah hugged her thinly clad arms around her waist and breathed in the heady scent of hot pink oleanders. Deliberately she forced one foot in front of the other. Moving quickly wasn't an option when the world occasionally tilted too far to the right. Beads of moisture on her forehead chilled her hot skin, making her shiver.

The bus driver had said two blocks—surely she'd come at least that far?

Suddenly off balance, Susannah stopped to steady herself. She focused her blurry eyes on the paper in her hand, peering to confirm that the numbers on the page were the same as those on the house. Her sluggish brain responded as if obscured by fog. She squinted for a second look.

This was it.

Susannah's heart sank a little lower. Such a grand home. How could she possibly walk into that perfectly manicured courtyard, knock on that elegant glass and wrought-iron door and ask Connie for help?

You're not worth helping, but you don't have a choice.

Nothing harder to stomach than the truth. Susannah knew that too well. She gritted her teeth, pushed open the gate and moved forward. Droplets of perspiration ran into her eyes, blurring her vision. She swiped them away with a quick brush of her hand, afraid to release the branches of the hedge for more than a second, lest she flop to the ground. She was cold, and yet she was so hot.

What was wrong with her?

Finally she stood at the entrance. Music floated out from the brightly lit house. Or maybe the melody was just stuck in her head.

Susannah lifted a hand and tapped gingerly, inhaling as the world spun faster.

The door opened, light and laughter flooding out.

"Yes?" A man's voice, rich and smooth, like butterscotch candy, flowed over her. It was hard to see his face, but light brown eyes gleamed through the dusk. "Can I help you?"

"Connie," Susannah whispered.

Then everything went black.

David Foster stared at the unconscious woman lying on his best friend Wade's doorstep. Wade's wife, Connie, always had someone stopping by, friends from the foster home where she'd once lived, acquaintances she'd met and offered to help, even total strangers who'd heard about her charities. This frail woman must fit into one of those categories.

But Connie and Wade were celebrating their return from Brazil with a houseful of guests. He didn't want to disturb them. As Wade's lawyer, David was accustomed to handling things for his friend. He decided he'd handle this guest, for now.

He bent and scooped the young woman into his arms.

"Who's that?" Darla asked. His little sister had a habit of soundlessly appearing at his elbow.

"I don't know," he murmured, leading the way to the study. "One of Connie's friends, I guess. She fainted. I think she's sick."

"Oh." Darla watched as he laid the young woman on the sofa. "Can I help, Davy?"

David smiled, brushed his hand over her shiny brown hair in a fond caress. Darla loved to help. Though nineteen, a skiing accident had left Darla with a brain injury that cut her mental age in half. David's goal in life was to make his sister's life as rich and happy as possible. It was becoming a challenge.

"Sure you can help, sweetie. Why don't you go in the bathroom over there and get a wet cloth?" he suggested. "You can wipe her forehead. She seems to have a fever."

"Okay."

Darla hurried to do as asked, her mood bright because of Connie's party. "Like this?" she asked him, dabbing the cloth on the woman's face.

"Very gently. That's good." He watched for a few moments. "She had a bag," he mused. "It must have dropped. Can you take care of her while I go look for it?"

"Yes." Darla hummed quietly as she gently removed the traces of dust and grime from the visitor's pale skin. Not that it mattered—their guest was gorgeous.

"I'll be right back." David hurried toward the front door, his mind filled with questions.

She was tiny, light as a feather. Her delicate features made him think of fashion magazine covers—thin, high cheekbones, full lips and wide-set eyes. She'd pulled her golden blond hair back and plaited it so it fell down her back, but little wisps had worked free to frame her face in delicate curls. He caught himself speculating what the color of her eyes would turn out to be when those incredible lashes lifted.

She's obviously needy, and your docket is full.

Boy, did he know that.

A denim backpack lay outside on the step. David bent to pick it up. Well used, even ragged. Like her clothes.

He carried the bag inside, quickening his step. Darla couldn't be left alone for long. He stepped into the room.

"You're Sleeping Beauty, aren't you?" his sister whispered as she slid her cloth over the girl's thin, ringless fingers. "You need Prince Charming to wake you up."

David knew what was coming. He tried to stall by taking the woman's pulse.

"She'll wake up in a few minutes, sis."

"No," Darla said, eyes darkening as her temper flared. "She needs you to kiss her, Davy. That's how Sleeping Beauty wakes up."

David sighed. Apparently he'd read her that particular fairy tale one too many times.

"It would be wrong of me to kiss her, Darla," he said firmly, ignoring the allure of full pink lips. "I don't know her. She wouldn't want a strange man to kiss her. Women don't like that."

"It's the only way to get her to wake up." Darla was growing agitated.

David closed the study door and prayed their visitor would soon rouse. He didn't want a scene at his friends' party. And Darla would make one. She'd grown used to getting her own way, and when she didn't, she tantrumed. That was the main reason she'd gone through so many caregivers in the past six months. None of the helpers he'd hired had been strong enough to stand up to Darla's iron will.

Like he was?

"Kiss her." Darla scowled at him, her mouth tight.

"No." David kept his voice firm. "It's no good getting angry, Darla. I'm not going to kiss her. This isn't a fairy tale, and she's not Sleeping Beauty. She's real and she might be quite ill. Look how she's shivering." He lifted a coverlet from the sofa and laid it over the small form.

"You have to kiss her." Darla stamped her foot. "I want you to." She swung out her hand. It connected with a lamp, which shattered against a table.

"Darla! Now you've broken Connie's lamp. Stop this immediately." David reached for her arm to keep her from wrecking anything else, but Darla was quick. She sidestepped him.

"Kiss her," she ordered, her face stormy as any thundercloud.

"Nobody's going to kiss me," a soft voice murmured. "And I wish you'd stop yelling. You sound like a spoiled brat."

Darla glowered at their visitor. Then she grinned. "Sometimes I am," she admitted shamelessly.

"Why? It's not very nice to live with people who are spoiled." The woman shifted the cover over her shoulders then swung her feet to the floor as she sat up. Her face paled a little and her fingers tightened on a sofa cushion.

"Easy," David murmured. "Not too fast. You fainted. Remember?"

"Unfortunately I do remember. What an entrance." She tilted her head back to rest it as she studied him.

Her eyes were a deep, vivid green. Their shadowed intensity reminded David of the Amazon forest—he'd once taken a trip there with Wade and their friend Jared. Before his world had become consumed by responsibility.

"My name is David Foster," he said. "This is my sister, Darla."

"I'm Susannah Wells. So this isn't Connie Ladden's home?" She looked defeated.

"Oh, yes. Connie and Wade *Abbot* live here," he assured her.

"They're having a party," Darla butted in. She frowned. "Did you come for the party? You don't have a party dress on. You're not supposed to come to a party if you don't dress nice," she chided.

"Darla." David frowned at her.

"She's only saying the truth. You're not supposed to show up at a party dressed as I am." Susannah smiled at him tentatively then turned to Darla. "But I didn't know it was a party, you see. Anyway, I don't have party dresses."

"Not even one?" Clearly this mystified Darla. "I have lots."

"Lucky you." Susannah frowned. "Maybe I should leave and come back tomorrow."

"You can't." Darla flopped down beside her.

Susannah blinked. "Why can't I?"

"'Cause you don't have any place to go. Do you?" Darla asked.

David tried to intervene but Susannah merely waved her hand at him to wait.

"How do you know that, Darla?" she asked, brows lowering.

"I'm a detective today."

"Oh." The visitor glanced at him, her confusion evident.

David shrugged but didn't speak.

"I'm Detective Darla Foster. You don't have any suitcases. All you have is a backpack." Darla trailed one finger over the frayed embroidery work on the bag. "If you had a hotel, you would go there and wash first. But you came here dirty. I washed your face." She lifted the wet washcloth off the floor and held it out to show the grime. "See?"

A ruby flush moved from the V of Susannah's neck up to her chin and over her thin cheeks.

"There was a wind," she muttered, avoiding David's gaze. "It was so dusty."

"It's none of our business," he assured her hastily, giving Darla a warning look. "Except that I don't think you're well. Should I call a doctor?"

"You actually know doctors who make house calls?" Her big eyes expressed incredulity.

"Dr. Boo came to my house. She asks too many questions." Darla's bottom lip jutted out. "Detectives don't like Dr. Boo."

"Dr. Boone," David clarified, interpreting Susannah's stare as a query. "Actually she's here. Shall I call her?"

"No." The word came out fast. Susannah donned a quick smile to cover. "I'm not very good with doctors. I'll be fine. I think I caught a little cold, that's all. But they never hang around for long."

"You're shivering." David didn't miss the way she hugged the coverlet around her shoulders as if craving warmth, or the way her stomach issued a noisy rumble. "And hungry, by the sounds of it. Shall I go get Connie?"

"Oh, please, I don't want to disturb her party." Susannah shook her head. "Can't I just stay here quietly until everyone's gone?"

"You don't want to go to the party?" Darla frowned, then grinned. "Me, neither," she declared. She patted Susannah's arm. "Let's have our own party. Davy, you get Silver," she ordered.

"Silver?" Susannah looked horrified. "I don't want money!'

"Silver is Wade's daughter." Darla giggled. "She's nice.'

"I think Connie took Silver up to bed a while ago." David held his breath, wondering if that would engender another explosion.

And that was exactly his problem. He worried too much about Darla's temper and not enough about insisting she modify her behavior. But it was so hard to be firm with her. She was his baby sister. She'd lost so much since the accident. All he wanted was to make her world easier, to see her happy.

Still, it was his job to take care of her, no matter what. Which meant that tomorrow David would start scouting the agencies—again—to find someone to be with his sister when he couldn't be.

Lowered voices drew him back to the present. Two heads, one dark, one blond, bent together as his sister laid out her plans for their impromptu party.

"Darla?" David waited until she lifted her head and smiled her dazzling smile at him. "I'm going to find something for Susannah to eat. Will you stay *here?*" He emphasized the word so she'd understand she wasn't to leave the study.

"Okay." Darla tore a piece of paper off the pad by the telephone and began scribbling. "Here's our order, Davy. Crackers and cheese and soup. Chicken soup. Eighty-six percent of doctors say chicken soup is an effective aid in treating cold and flu."

Darla had a knack for reciting television commercials verbatim.

"Cold and flu—is that what I have?" Susannah asked, tongue in cheek. "How do you know?"

"I'm a nurse. We just know." Darla pulled the cover tighter around her patient's shoulders.

David hid his smile at Susannah's surprise.

"I thought you were a detective," he said.

"Not anymore." Darla glared at him. "Food, Davy. This child is starving," she said in her bossy grandmother voice.

"Yes, ma'am." He choked back his laughter. Darla had always been able to make him laugh. He headed for the door. "I'll be right back." He thought he heard a giggle from the blond woman before he closed the door, but it was quickly smothered.

David went searching for Connie and caught her between guests.

"There's a woman in the study, a Susannah Wells," he began, but got no further.

"Really? Suze? How wonderful." Connie beamed with happiness. It faded a little as she glanced around the room. "We're about to eat dinner. I can't leave right now." She thought a moment. "Bring her to the table, will you, David? I'll get another place set."

Before Connie could continue, David stopped her.

"I don't think that's a good idea," he said softly. "I don't think she's well. She fainted when I opened the door and she's been shivering ever since."

"Oh, dear." Connie looked distracted. "Cora just gave me the nod. I need to get everyone seated."

"Then go ahead. Darla and I will keep Ms. Susannah entertained until you're free." David smiled at her. "Don't worry. Darla has everything under control. She's a nurse."

"Ah." Connie grinned in understanding and stood on her tiptoes to kiss his cheek. "What would we do without Darla, David?"

"I don't know," he answered her, perfectly serious. "Go enjoy dinner and don't worry about your friend. I'll look after her."

"You always look after everyone." Connie touched his cheek. "Thank you for all you do for us. You're a dear."

David watched her hurry away. He couldn't help but envy Connie. She and Wade shared the kind of home he'd always wanted—one filled with love and joy, hope and the laughter of friends and family. But he shook himself out of it. Having a family was a dream he'd given up.

For Darla.

He escaped to the kitchen. A whisper of concern that Darla might cause problems lingered at the back of his mind as he hurriedly filled a tray and carried it to the study. He hadn't gotten what she'd asked for, but she would have to manage. He pushed open the study door—and froze.

"You could marry Davy. He would look after you. He looks after me." Darla's bright voice dropped. "He had a girlfriend. They were going to get married, but she didn't want me. She wanted Davy to send me away."

David almost groaned. How had she found out? He'd been so careful—

"I'm sure your brother is very nice, Darla. And I'm glad he's taking care of you. But I don't want to marry him. I don't want to marry anyone," Susannah said. "I only came to Connie's to see if I could stay here for a while."

"But Davy needs someone to love him. Somebody else but me." Darla's face crumpled, the way it always did before she lost her temper. David was about to step forward when Susannah reached out and hugged his sister.

"Thank you for offering, Darla. You're very generous. I think your brother is lucky to have you love him." Susannah brushed the bangs from Darla's sad face. "If I end up staying with Connie, I promise I'll see you lots. We could go to that playground you talked about—" Susannah suddenly lurched up from the sofa and stumbled toward the bathroom. The door slammed closed.

"What's wrong?" Darla jumped to her feet. She saw

him and rushed over. "What's wrong with her, Davy? Did I do something?"

"No, sweetie. You didn't do anything." He set the tray on a nearby table, then hugged Darla close. "I told you. She's sick."

"But I don't want Susannah to be sick. I want us to be friends and do things together." Tears welled in Darla's brown eyes. "Susannah doesn't think I'm dumb. She talks to me like you do, Davy."

David could hardly stand the plaintive tone in his sister's voice. But he dared not promise Darla anything. Not until he'd learned a lot more about Susannah Wells.

As he hugged Darla, the sounds of retching penetrated the silence. Susannah sounded really ill. Maybe he should have ignored her wishes and called the doctor in anyway.

"Davy?" Darla peered up at him, her eyes glossy from tears. "Do you think she's going to die like Mama and Papa?"

"No, honey. Susannah's just sick. But she'll get better." He squeezed her shoulders, wishing he could make everything right with Darla's world.

A moment later the bathroom door opened and Susannah emerged, paler than before, if that was even possible. She sat on the sofa gingerly, as if afraid she'd jar something loose.

"I'm sorry," she whispered. "I shouldn't have come."

"Of course you should have come." Connie breezed into the room and wrapped Susannah in her arms. "I'm so glad to see you, Suze. But you're ill." She leaned back to study the circles of red now dotting Susannah's cheeks. "I'll call the doctor."

"No."

David noted Susannah's quick intake of breath,

the way she vehemently shook her head as her fingers clenched the sofa cushion. He wondered again why she was so nervous.

"But honey, you're obviously unwell. Maybe you have a virus."

Susannah began to laugh, but tears soon fell and the laughter turned to sobs. "I don't have a virus, Connie." She risked a quick look at David.

He understood immediately. He grasped Darla's hand.

"We'll leave you two alone."

"No!" Darla jerked away from him and sat down beside Susannah. "I want to help my friend. Can I help you?" she asked quietly, sliding her fingers into Susannah's.

David had never seen his sister bond with anyone like this. He prayed Susannah wouldn't reject her offer of friendship.

"You already have helped me, Darla." Susannah smiled. "You looked after me and helped me the way a very good friend would, even though I hardly know you."

"I know you," Darla insisted. "You're Sleeping Beauty."

"I'm not really." Susannah caressed Darla's cheek. She glanced at him, then Connie. "I'm just an idiot who's made another huge mistake."

"Davy says everybody makes mistakes. He said that's how we learn." Darla faced Connie. "I made a mistake and broke your lamp. I'm sorry."

"That's okay, honey. You and I will go shopping for a new one." Connie smiled her forgiveness, then turned back to Susannah. "Can you tell me what's wrong, Suze?

Because you're very pale and I still think you need to see a doctor."

"I've already seen one." The blond head dipped. "I know what's wrong with me."

"Tell me and we'll do whatever it takes to get you well," Connie promised.

"If only it were that easy," Susannah whispered.

"There's me and Davy and Connie and Wade and Silver. That's lots of people to help." Darla twisted, trying to peer into Susannah's face. "We can all help you. That's what friends do."

David had to smile at the certainty in his sister's voice. But his smile quickly died.

"I'm pregnant." The words burst out of Susannah in a rush. Then she lifted her head and looked him straight in the eye, as if awaiting his condemnation.

But it wasn't condemnation David felt. It was hurt. He'd prayed so long, so hard, for a family, a wife, a child. And he'd lost all chance of that—not once, but twice.

How could God deny him the longing of his heart, yet give this homeless, ill woman a child she was in no way prepared to care for?

"Come on, Darla," he said. "We're going home now. Connie and Susannah need to talk. Alone."

Darla must have heard intransigence in his voice because she didn't argue. She leaned over and kissed both women on the cheek, whispered something to Susannah, then placidly followed him from the room. She walked home beside him in silence, peeking at him from time to time. It was only when they'd stepped through the front door that Darla finally spoke.

"I know what it means, Davy. Susannah's going to have a baby."

"Yes." He felt horrible about his attitude, but he just

didn't want to get involved with Connie's friend. He had enough responsibility with Darla. He couldn't—wouldn't—take on any more.

"Is it hard to have a baby?" she asked.

"Yes. I guess so."

"Then we have to help Susannah, don't we? That's what the Bible says." Darla took his hand and held it between hers. "She's my friend, and I want to help her."

"I don't think there's much that we can do, sis." Brain injury or not, Darla had always tried to fix the world. David loved that. Loved her. "It's not our problem."

"Yes, it is our problem. We have to show love." Darla let go of his hand and stepped back. Her face was set in stern lines, her dark eyes glowing with the unyielding resolve he'd run into before. "I'm going to help Susannah. I'm going to ask God to show me how."

Then she turned and walked to her room, determination in every step.

David went into his study but he didn't turn on the lights. Instead he stood in the dark, thinking. Finally he could contain his hurt no longer.

"I don't want to take on anyone else's problems, God," he whispered. "I was Silver's guardian for four years while Wade worked in South America. When Dad died, I took over his law firm, and then managed Mom's care until she passed away. Then Darla had her accident and it was up to me again. I can't take on any more."

"I'll be good, Davy," Darla whispered.

He whirled around, saw her standing in the doorway with tears coursing down her cheeks and cursed his stupidity.

"Oh, Darla, honey, I didn't mean—"

"I promise I won't be bad anymore. I won't yell or

break things or be nasty, if we could have Susannah look after me. Please?" She stood in her white cotton nightgown, a penitent child where a woman should have been. She'd lost so much.

His heart ached to make her world better. But not this way.

"Sweetie, I don't think Susannah is going to be able to work. I think she'll have to rest and get well."

"For a little while, till she's not sick. But then Susannah will want to work. She told me she came to see if Connie could help her get a job." Darla dragged on his arm. "Ms. Evans said she isn't ever coming back here to stay with me again, so we have a job, Davy. Please, could we get Susannah?"

David had never been able to deny his sister her heart's desire. Not since the day she'd been born. Certainly not since her accident. But David couldn't promise this. Darla took every spare moment he had and then some. He had to be her buffer, protect her and make sure her world was safe and secure. He couldn't take on the responsibility for a pregnant woman, too. He just couldn't take on another obligation for anything or anyone else.

Can't or won't? his conscience probed.

"Please, Davy?"

"I'm not saying yes," he warned. "I'm saying I'll think about it. But don't get your hopes up, Darla, because I don't believe Susannah will want to do it."

And I don't want her here. I don't want to be responsible if she works too hard or you cause her problems and that child is jeopardized. I don't want more responsibility.

"Thank you, Davy." Darla flung her arms around him and hugged him as hard as she could.

"I haven't said Susannah can come, remember."

"I know." She tipped her head back and grinned like the old Darla would have. "But I'm going to pray God will change your mind." She kissed him, then raced toward the kitchen. "I didn't have dinner. I'm hungry."

Darla's faith.

David wished his own was as strong.

Chapter Two

"So you thought you were married to this man?" Connie said.

"Nick. Yes." Susannah nodded.

"But—"

"I know it sounds stupid and gullible," Susannah muttered and hung her head. "He said he didn't want a fuss, that he wanted our wedding to be just us, private and intimate."

"But to lie about marriage—I am so sorry." Connie touched her hand in wordless sympathy.

"So am I—sorry that I was so dumb. Nick arranged everything that I asked for—the minister, the church, everything. But it wasn't real. None of it was." Susannah pushed away the rest of the soup David had brought. She shook her head. "I thought Nick loved me. I guess I should have known better."

"Why? When you're in love, you do trust the one you love." Connie's fingers smoothed hers. "That's natural, exactly how God meant love to be."

"Only God didn't mean love for me." Guilt settled on Susannah for ruining her friend's party. "Shouldn't you go back to your guests?"

"I told them an emergency had arisen."

"I'm an emergency? Yuk." Susannah made a face.

"Just like the old days, huh?" Connie teased. She shook her head. "Don't worry. They're friends and well used to my 'emergencies.' Wade will take care of them."

"Is he nice?" Susannah asked softly, studying her friend's glowing face with a twinge of envy.

"Wade is—wonderful." Connie's face radiated happiness.

"How did you meet?"

"Silver is Wade's daughter. Wade had to leave her here while he worked in South America. David was her guardian. He hired me to be Silver's nanny."

"How romantic. Like Cinderella." Susannah thought Darla would have loved that.

"Not at first. When Wade came home he was nothing like I expected. But God knew what he was doing when he put us together. We were married a year ago." Connie held out her hand. "My engagement ring was Wade's mother's."

"It's beautiful." Susannah thought of the cheap gold circlet she'd tucked into her bag. Nick had promised he'd get something nicer later on. Another lie. "Nick died and I didn't have anywhere else to go."

"Oh, Suze, I'm so glad you came here. You were only seventeen when you ran away from our foster home. What have you been doing?" Connie asked, her voice grave. "I called home several times, but Mom said she didn't know where you'd gone."

"I got in with the wrong group and went to Los Angeles. It took me a while to get my head on straight, but eventually I got a job in a nursing home. That's where

I met Nick." She inhaled to ease the constriction in her throat. No more tears.

Connie squeezed her fingers. "How did you find me?"

"I finally phoned Mom day before yesterday."

"She misses you." Connie's eyes blazed with sympathy.

"I miss her, too." Susannah sniffed. "I was stupid to run away. So stupid."

"Everybody makes mistakes."

"Even you?" Susannah asked, glancing around.

"Especially me." Connie laughed. "I'll tell you later about my mistakes." Her voice grew serious. "But what about the baby, Suze? When are you due?"

"April. Around Easter."

"An Easter baby."

Susannah gulped. "I'm on my own and I have about two nickels to rub together. I guess, first of all, I need to find a job. Do you know of any?"

"First of all you need to get better," Connie said in her familiar "mother" tone. "Do you want to keep your baby?"

"I don't think any child would want a mother like me." She deliberately didn't look at Connie.

"But you'd make a wonderful mother!" her friend protested.

"Hardly," Susannah scoffed. "Look how I messed up my own family. I'm so not the poster woman for motherhood."

"You were nine the day they brought you to our foster home. I told you then and I'll tell you again, *you* did not break up your family, Suze. Nothing you did caused your father to leave you, or your mother to start drinking. And you did not start that fire." Connie tucked a finger under her chin and forced her to look up.

Susannah couldn't stop the tears. "Why did God let this happen to me, Connie?"

"Oh, sweetheart." Connie wrapped comforting arms around her shoulders and hugged her close, rocking back and forth as she had when Susannah was younger.

"I feel like He hates me," Susannah sobbed.

"God? No way." Connie let go and leaned back. "Listen to me, kiddo, and hear me well. God does not hate you. He loves you more than you could ever imagine."

"But I've messed up—"

"There are no 'buts' where God is concerned. He loves you. Period." Connie pressed the tendrils away from Susannah's face, then cupped her cheeks and peered straight into her eyes. "God has a plan. He's going to work all of this out for your benefit."

"You sound so sure."

"I am sure. Positive." Connie smiled. "But until He shows us the next step, I have the perfect guest room upstairs. You'll stay as long as you need to. Now finish that soup and try to swallow a few of the crackers," she insisted. "You're thinner now than you were when you first came to North Dakota, and you were a stick then. Eat."

"Still as bossy," Susannah teased, her heart swelling at the relief of being able to count on a friend.

"Still needing bossing," Connie shot back, laughing. "You need taking care of, and I'm just the person to do it." She watched while Susannah ate. "What was Darla saying about Sleeping Beauty?"

Susannah shrugged but couldn't stop her blush. "I passed out on the doorstep. Her brother carried me in here. When I came to, she was demanding he kiss me, like Sleeping Beauty." Susannah crunched another cracker, enjoying the feeling of having enough to satisfy her hunger. It had been ages since she'd been able to eat her fill.

"She loves that story." Connie smiled fondly.

"Darla is a bit old for fairy tales," Susannah mused. "Something's wrong with her, right?"

"She had a skiing accident." Connie's voice filled with sadness. "It happened a few months after her mother died. Their father was already gone so David had to handle everything. He's been looking after her the best he can, but it's been a challenge for him."

"What do you mean?" Susannah struggled to decipher the cautious tone in Connie's voice.

"Well, David was engaged. Twice."

"Oh." Not much wonder, Susannah thought. He was very good-looking.

"Each time his fiancées backed out because of Darla."

"They wanted him to dump her into some home?" Indignation filled Susannah. "Typical."

"Why do you say that, Suze?"

"It was like that where I worked," Susannah fumed. "So often the seniors were seen as burdens because they took a little extra time and attention, or couldn't remember as well."

"Well, in Darla's case, David's fiancées might have had a point," Connie said, her voice quiet.

"Oh?" Susannah frowned. "Why?"

"Darla has had—" Connie paused "—difficulty adjusting to her world since the accident."

"But surely she goes to a program of some sort?" Susannah asked.

"She does. The problem is Darla. She has trouble working with anyone. Her temper gets very bad. I'm sure that's what happened with my lamp." Connie inclined her head toward the shattered glass.

"When I came to, she was yelling." Susannah frowned. "But she didn't act up when I was speaking with her. She was sweet and quite charming."

"That's the way she is, until someone doesn't do as she wants. Then she balks and makes a scene. It's part of her brain injury. She's had a number of workers try to teach her stronger self-control." Connie made a face. "With little success, so far. They keep quitting."

"Well, maybe David hasn't found the right people to work with her," Susannah said. "He seemed kind of frustrated by her."

"Maybe he is," Connie agreed, "but he devotes himself to his sister."

"To the exclusion of everything else?" Was that why he looked so tired?

"Yes, sometimes. David is convinced it's his duty to his parents to ensure Darla's happiness, even if he has to sacrifice his own." Connie pulled a vacuum hose from a cupboard and cleaned up the shards of glass before tucking the lampshade into a closet.

"Aren't you mad about the lamp?" Susannah asked curiously.

"It was just a thing." Connie loaded the used dishes onto the tray. "People are more important than things. Come."

Connie opened a door that led to a staircase. Susannah followed her, curious to see the rest of this lovely house.

"We'll sneak up to your room this way." Connie shot her a conspiratorial grin.

Their footsteps were muffled by thickly carpeted stairs. Connie grasped her hand and led her to a beautiful room tucked under the eaves.

"This used to be my room," she said. Her face reflected a flurry of emotions as she sank onto the window seat. "I spent a lot of time right here, praying."

"Are you happy, Connie?" Susannah asked, sitting beside her. "Truly?"

"Happier than I ever imagined I'd be." Connie hugged her. "You will be, too, Suze. But you have to give God time to work things out for you. You have to have faith that He has great things in store for your future."

"That's hard, given my past," Susannah muttered.

"That's when it's most important to read your Bible and pray," Connie murmured. "You have a lot of decisions to make. But you don't have to rush. You can stay right here, get well and figure things out in your own time."

"Is it hard—being a mother?" The question slipped out in spite of her determination not to ask.

But the prospect of motherhood scared her silly.

"You're worried about the baby, aren't you, Suze. Why?" Connie moved to sit on the bed, patting the space beside her. When Susannah sat down, she hugged her close. "What's really bothering you?"

"My role model for motherhood wasn't exactly nurturing. Nothing mattered to my mother more than her next drink." She heard the resentment in her own voice but couldn't control it. "Nothing."

"Suze, honey, you can't hold on to the bitterness."

"Can't I?" Susannah opened her bag and pulled out her wallet. She flipped it to two pictures nestled inside. "They're dead, Connie. Because of me."

"No."

"Yes." Susannah nodded. "I should have been there."

"Then you would have died, too." Connie gripped her hand.

"But if only I hadn't chosen—"

"The fire wasn't your fault, Susannah." Connie's soft voice hardened. "No matter what your mother said when you were a kid."

Susannah had gone round and round this argument in her head for years. But nothing erased the little voice of blame in the back of her brain. Her hand rested for an instant on her stomach.

"A new life," Connie murmured. "Hard to wrap your mind around it?"

"Very," Susannah agreed with a grimace. "Even harder to imagine coping."

"You'll do fine," Connie assured her.

"It's easy for you to say that. You spent all those years in our foster home caring for everybody else. I don't know anything about caring for a baby, except that you need to feed it and change it." Just saying that made Susannah feel helpless. "What if it gets sick?"

"Then you'll get help." Connie patted her shoulder. "One thing I've learned with Silver is that there are no easy answers, no recipe you can follow. You do your best, pray really hard and have faith that God will answer. And He does. David told me that when he first hired me."

"Really?" So David Foster was a man of faith, too.

"David is one of the good guys. My husband is another. So is their friend Jared." Connie smiled with pride. "They're the kind of men who do the right thing, no matter what. Integrity. They have it in spades."

Susannah couldn't dislodge the image of the tall dark-haired man with the slow spreading grin that started with a slight lift at the corners of his mouth, followed by a gradual widening until it reached his toffee eyes. David Foster had the kind of smile that took forever to get where it was going, but once it got there, it took your breath.

"A lawyer with integrity," she mused. "How novel."

Connie drew back the quilt and patted a pillow. "Come on, into bed. Your eyelids are drooping. Rest. We'll talk again whenever you're ready."

"Did I say thank you?" Tears swelled Susannah's throat.

"What are sisters for?" Connie hugged her. "Don't worry about anything, Suze. You're here now. Relax. In due time you can start planning for the future. Just remember—you're not alone."

A moment later she was gone, the door whispering closed behind her. Susannah stood up, tiredness washing over her. Then she spied the bathroom door.

Five minutes later she was up to her neck in bubbles in a huge tub, enjoying the relaxing lavender fragrance as jets pulsed water over her weary flesh.

Are You really watching out for me, God?

She thought over the past months and the tumble from joy to despair that she'd experienced. Unbidden, thoughts of David's troubles rose. How difficult to lose both your parents, and then the sister you'd known and loved. They had that in common—loss.

Susannah hadn't said anything to Darla or Connie, but when David had carried her into the house, she had come to, for a second. And in that moment, she *had* felt like Sleeping Beauty. Awakening to a whole new perspective on life.

Which was really stupid. She didn't want anything to do with love. Certainly not the romantic fairy-tale kind—that only led to disappointment and pain.

Susannah Wells had never had a fairy-tale life and she doubted it was about to start now, just because a nice man and his sister had cared for her. She didn't deserve a picture-perfect life.

And you won't have one. You're pregnant, Susannah. David Foster won't give you a second look.

Not that she wanted him to. Depend on yourself. She'd learned that lesson very well a long time ago.

Wearied by all the questions that had no answers, Susannah rose, drained the tub and prepared for bed. But when she finally climbed in between the sheets, she felt wide awake. She pulled open the drawer of the nightstand to search for something to read. A Bible lay there.

She picked it up with no idea of where to start reading. She let it fall open on the bed. Isaiah 43.

I, I am the One who forgives all your sins, for My sake, I will not remember your sins.

God forgave her? That's what Connie had said. But maybe it was only an accident that she was reading these words. Susannah closed the Bible, let it fall open again.

2 Corinthians.

God is the Father who is full of mercy and all comfort. He comforts us every time we have trouble, so when others have trouble, we can comfort them with the same comfort God gives us.

So many times she'd asked herself, where is God? According to this, He was right here, comforting her with Connie's house. He was the father who didn't walk out when life got rough.

A flicker of hope burst into flame inside Susannah's heart.

Maybe God could forgive the stupid choices she'd

made. Maybe…but she doubted it. She wasn't like Connie—good and smart and worth saving.

God had let her get duped by Nick. Why?

Because she wasn't worth loving. Her whole life was proof of that.

Susannah let her tears flow far into the night.

Chapter Three

David screeched to a halt in front of his home and jumped out of the car.

"I'm sorry, Mr. Foster. I only went to get Darla a drink because she said she was thirsty. When I came back, she was gone." The caregiver wrung her hands. "I've looked everywhere. She's not in the house or the yard."

"Okay. Okay." He forced his brain to focus. "Show me what she was doing."

"Here."

He studied the reams of pictures Darla had drawn. Nothing made sense to him.

"What were you talking about?" he asked.

"Actually I was reading."

"Reading what?" Suspicions rose.

"*Sleeping Beauty*. From that big book she likes so much." The woman pointed. "I tried to read something else, but she wouldn't listen.

Two weeks of Darla nagging him to visit Connie's.

Suddenly it all made sense to David.

"Wait here a moment, would you please?" He picked up the phone and dialed, chagrined when Susannah

Wells answered. "This is David Foster. By chance, did Darla walk over there?"

"Connie is just now calling your office," Susannah explained. "We were having lunch by the pool when Darla showed up. She was quite upset. Connie didn't want to make it worse so she included her in our lunch. Not that you need to worry," she added.

"Why's that?"

"Darla calmed down immediately once we got her busy. Connie has tons of puzzles. Darla seems fascinated by them, too."

Puzzles? Since when?

"I'll be over in a few minutes to pick her up," he said. "I'm sorry she bothered you."

"Darla's no bother at all," Susannah said. She paused, then spoke slowly, thoughtfully. "It would be nice if she could stay for a while, though, if that won't upset your plans."

Ha! David's plans had gone on hold the moment he'd received the call.

"I'm afraid I've been at loose ends, taking up too much of Connie's time," Susannah explained. "Having Darla here would free Connie to attend to her own issues. She wouldn't have to keep babysitting me."

"You're feeling better?" Not that he wanted to know. He'd spent hours shoving the memory of Susannah's face out of his brain.

"Oh, yes. Much recovered." She chuckled. "Especially with Darla here. She's got a wicked sense of humor."

"Mmm." What was he supposed to say to that? "Well, I'll come and get her out of your hair."

"Really, it's not— Oh, here's Connie."

"David?" Connie sounded breathless.

"Sorry for the invasion," he apologized.

"Invasion? Darla's like a refreshing breeze off the mountains. Which, given today's heat, I could use. This is not autumn in Tucson as I've known it." She chuckled.

"Hang around, you'll get used to it." He swallowed. "Connie—"

She cut him off.

"David, I was thinking—" He could almost hear the wheels grinding in Connie's head. "Couldn't Darla stay? Susannah and I are enjoying the visit as much as she. In fact, I've just had the most wonderful idea."

"Oh?" He glanced at his watch, not really listening to Connie's plan. Ten minutes before his next client arrived in his office. Could he get back in ten minutes?

"…Susannah would be great at it. They really connect."

"I'm sorry, Connie," he interrupted. "What did you say?"

"I said, why don't you ask Susannah about caring for Darla after school? She has her certification as a special care aide. And she's very level-headed. They get along so well. I'm sure Darla would love it."

"I don't think a pregnant woman—"

"Don't be silly. This is October and Susannah's not due until Easter. I think it would be perfect," Connie enthused. She lowered her voice. "Susannah really needs a job, David. Working with Darla is taxing but it would only be for a few hours a day and it would keep her mind occupied. The hours Darla spends at her school would also give Susannah some time on her own."

David hated the whole idea. He didn't want a pregnant woman in his employ, someone else to be responsible for. Especially someone he was faintly attracted to.

Faintly?

David shut off the mocking laughter in his head and refocused. His sister had to have someone, and clearly the woman the agency had sent over wasn't going to work out. Again.

"Will you consider it?" Connie asked. "Please?"

"I can't decide this right now. I left the office in a rush and I've got an urgent appointment in a few minutes." David thought for a moment. "Could Darla stay there for the afternoon, just till I get home? Then I'm going to have to talk to her. This can't happen again."

"I'll make sure she stays. You go do your work. We'll be fine," Connie insisted. "But promise me you'll think about my suggestion. It would be so perfect."

"Connie, Darla is bigger than Susannah. And stronger, judging by what I saw. She could hurt your friend. Not intentionally, but she does lash out."

"But that's the funny thing. She hasn't with Susannah. Maybe because of the baby, I don't know." Connie sighed. "I know how you like to dot all the *i*'s, David. Go back to your office. Think on it. We'll be here."

"Thanks. You're a good friend, Connie." David hung up and wasted a few minutes musing on the idea.

"Am I fired?"

He blinked and saw the helper he'd hired staring at him.

"Because if I'm not, I quit. I can't do this. She's— violent."

"She just gets a little frustrated. I'm sorry if Darla scared you. Here." He handed her a wad of money. "That should cover your expenses. Thanks a lot."

By the time David returned to his office, his father's former client was antsy and David had his work cut out assuring the high-profile man that his case wouldn't suffer just because his father wasn't handling it. David worked steadily until he suddenly noticed the office was quiet and the clock said ten to six.

He was so far behind he could have used another three hours to catch up. But no way was he going to add to Connie's responsibilities by shirking his. Traffic was backed up and by the time he arrived on their street the sun had long since dipped below the craggy red Rincon Mountain tips.

"I'm so sorry," he began as the door opened. He stopped. Susannah. "Hello." She looked infinitely better than she had last time. In fact, she glowed.

"Hello, yourself." She didn't smile. "We're about to sit down to dinner."

"Then I won't bother you." He could feel the ice in her voice. "If you'll call Darla?"

"No, I won't." She stepped forward and pulled the door closed behind her, forcing him to take a step back. "You can't make her leave now."

"Why not?" The peremptory tone of her voice confused him.

"Darla's spent a huge amount of time helping prepare this meal," Susannah informed him. "It's only fair she should get to enjoy it."

"I'm not sure this is about fairness. But—"

She cut him off.

"Look, I get that you don't like me, that you think I'm some kind of a tramp. It was evident in the way you looked at me when I told Connie I was pregnant." Her face flushed red but she didn't stop glaring at him. "Fine. No problem. But this isn't about me."

If that's what she thought, her perceptions were way off. David had lost valuable billing time in the past two weeks thinking about Susannah Wells, and not one thought had been negative.

"Did you hear me?" she asked, frowning.

"This isn't about you," he repeated, noting the way the porch light reflected the emerald sparks in her eyes. The deep hollows under her cheeks had filled out a little and that pallid, sickly look was completely gone. Her blond hair shone like a swath of hammered gold as it tumbled down her back.

"It isn't about you, either. It's about Darla. She's tried very hard to make up for worrying you by leaving your house without telling anyone. Helping with dinner is her way of making up." Susannah lowered her voice as the door creaked open. "Can't you let her have that much?"

She made it sound like he was some kind of an ogre. David fumed. But he kept his lips buttoned because Darla's dark head appeared in the doorway.

"Can we stay for dinner, Davy? Connie invited, I didn't ask." His sister stood in front of him, hands clasped at her waist as she waited. She looked different and it took David a minute to figure out why. Her hair. It had been styled in a way that showed off her pretty eyes.

"Do you deserve to stay?" he asked, waiting for her to blow up.

But Darla simply shook her head.

"No, I don't," she murmured. "I promised not to leave the house without asking, and I broke my promise. I'm sorry, Davy."

"Are you really?" he asked, suspicious of the meek tone in her voice. He glanced at Susannah but she was watching Darla, her face an expressionless mask.

"I really am." Darla peeked at Susannah who gave a slight nod. "I got mad because Ms. Matchett said my fairy-tale book was silly. We argued, and she said I was a dummy." Her bottom lip trembled, but after a moment she collected herself. "I didn't like her calling me that so I left. But I shouldn't have. I'm sorry, Davy."

His hands tightened into balls of anger. Dummy. The one put-down Darla hated most of all. No wonder she'd run.

"I was really scared, Darla," he said quietly. "I didn't know if you'd been hurt or got lost or what had happened. I was ready to call the police."

"The police?" Her eyes grew huge, then flared. "But I didn't do anything wrong!" She stamped her foot.

Susannah cleared her throat. Darla's entire demeanor altered.

"I'm sorry, Davy," she said. "I did do something wrong. I know it. And I won't do that ever again. I promise. Okay?"

Those big brown eyes—they always got to him. Peering up at him so adoringly from the first day he'd seen her in her bassinet. The innocence was still there.

"Okay. I forgive you."

She threw her arms around him in an exuberant hug and nearly squeezed the breath out of him. Behind her, Susannah hid her grin behind her hand.

"Thank you, Davy." Darla was all smiles now. "So can we stay for dinner? I helped," she said proudly.

"If Connie says it's okay," he muttered, knowing he'd been bested.

"She will."

He watched his sister and Susannah share a grin before Darla hurried into the house.

"She was very hurt by that Matchett person's comment," Susannah murmured.

He nodded.

"She hates to be called dumb." He studied her. "What did you say to her?"

"What makes you think I said anything?" She preceded him into the house.

"Connie seems to think the two of you have developed some kind of rapport." He couldn't help but notice the way Susannah's face tightened.

"You don't like that, do you?" she challenged. "You don't think someone like me should be anywhere around Darla."

"I don't think that at all," he argued.

"Darla is a lot smarter than you give her credit for, Mr. Foster."

"My name is David."

Susannah paused in the foyer, her face serious. "Your sister is very smart, David. She craves your attention. She feels alone and she desperately wants to please you." She tilted her head to one side, watching him. "I'm no psychiatrist, but I think Darla wants to prove to you that she's good at something. Hence the reciting of commercials and such."

"That's—interesting," he said.

"She could do so many things." Susannah's voice grew intense. "But she says you won't let her try. You're afraid she'll hurt herself. That's hard on her."

"Uh—"

"You don't think I know what I'm talking about. I get that. I guess I wouldn't listen to me, either. I don't have any credentials and I'm not exactly a walking advertisement for responsibility. But please, don't write off Darla's ideas too quickly. That's worse to her than being called dumb."

She'd put her hand on his arm as she spoke, imploring him to listen. David glanced at it. Susannah only then seemed aware of what she'd done and hurriedly jerked her hand away.

"Never mind," she whispered and hurried toward the others.

All through dinner David kept watch over his sister and the woman she seemed to adore. Darla told Susannah all about the pottery she'd made in her therapy classes, but it was the first time David had heard that she missed working with clay.

Or that she didn't like the outfit she wore. His choice.

Susannah Wells had been busy.

"Aren't they great together?" Connie sat by him in the family room, watching Susannah and Darla with Silver outside in the courtyard. "Darla has a way with flowers, David. She repotted several cacti with Hornby this afternoon and you know he never lets anyone help him do that."

Just yesterday David had refused to let Darla weed the flower garden, afraid she'd hurt herself on the prickly thorns of the cholla.

Was Susannah right? Was he holding her back?

No. Susannah was full of advice, but she wasn't the one who had to rescue Darla when something bad happened, or calm her when life didn't go her way.

"She's been asking Susannah questions about the baby all day." Connie chuckled. "She's very excited."

"Connie." David frowned as he struggled to find the right words. "I'm sure Susannah is a nice person. And I'm guessing something bad landed her here, but—"

"Something bad? You could say that," Connie said, her voice harsh. "She married a guy she thought loved her. When he found out she was pregnant, he told her they weren't actually married at all and he kicked her out." She smiled grimly. "Susannah has a long history of those she trusts letting her down, so much so that she doesn't believe she's worthy of love."

"I'm sorry." He didn't know what else to say.

"Give her a chance, David," Connie pleaded. "Susannah's smart, she's funny, but most of all, she is good for Darla. Isn't that the kind of caregiver you want?"

What he wanted was a stranger, someone with no ties to him, who would come in, do her job and leave without affecting him. Susannah was beautiful, he'd already noticed that. And she was pregnant.

There would be complications if he hired her. Lots of them.

I don't have to get personally involved, other than making sure she's medically fit for work and that she can handle Darla. There's no need for me to treat Susannah Wells as anything more than an employee.

Somewhere in the recesses of his brain David heard mocking laughter.

Like he hadn't already noticed her intense eyes, fine-limbed figure or model-perfect face.

"David?" Connie's voice prodded him back to reality.

Laughter, sweet and carefree, floated into the family room from the courtyard. Susannah. She stood in a patch of light, gilded by the silvery beams, her delicate features faintly pink from the exertion of tossing a ball. She looked the same age as Darla.

"How old is she?" he asked.

"Twenty-two. Just." Connie frowned. "Does her age matter?"

Three years older than Darla. And about to be a mother.

"Come on, Darla," Susannah cheered. "You can throw it all the way from there. I know you can."

And Darla did.

"I'll give her a trial period of two weeks," David told Connie. "If she finds the work too hard or Darla too difficult, she can back out. I just hope Darla doesn't change her mind and blow up."

"I don't think that's going to happen, David." Connie laughed. "Just look at the two of them."

Susannah and Darla stood together, arms around each other's waists as they watched Silver dive into the pool. Susannah said something to Darla, who was now clad in a swimsuit. When had that happened?

David jumped to his feet. Darla was scared of water. She panicked when it closed over her head and after being rescued, always took hours of calming. And then came the nightmares.

"No!" he yelled.

But he was too late. Darla jumped into the pool. The water closed over her body. David rushed outside, furious that he hadn't been paying enough attention. He saw her black swimsuit sink to the bottom and yanked off his shirt.

"Wait." Susannah pulled on his arm. "Give her a chance."

"She hates it," he hissed. "She freezes underwater."

But after what seemed an eternity, Darla resurfaced and began to move, pushing herself across the pool until she reached the other side. She grabbed the side, gasping for air but grinning.

"I did it." She pumped her fist in the air. "Did you see, Susannah? I did it."

"I knew you would." Susannah smiled at her, watching as Darla darted through the shallow water to chase

Silver. "You have to believe in her, David," she murmured. "Otherwise, how will she believe in herself?"

Then Susannah turned away, found a lounger and sank into it, her attention wholly focused on the pair in the pool.

She was right.

That was the thing that shocked David the most. This girl, seven years his junior with no training, not only saw Darla's potential but helped his sister find it.

He walked toward her.

"I'd like to offer you a job," he said. "But only if you are checked out by a doctor and he okays you to work with Darla. It would be only a few hours a day with perhaps some time on Saturdays." He told her how much he was willing to pay.

"There's a catch, isn't there?" Susannah said after a long silence, during which she studied him with those intense green eyes. "What is it?"

David didn't hesitate.

"Every activity you plan has to be approved by me," he told her.

"Every one?" She smiled. "Wow, you are a control freak, aren't you?"

"I insist on keeping my sister safe," he said firmly. "That's my condition."

"I see." Susannah's scrutiny didn't diminish. After a long silence she frowned. "Did you ever consider that you might be keeping her too safe?"

"No." He wasn't going to start out with her questioning his rules. "I'd like to start with a trial period of two weeks. Do you want the job or not?"

She kept him waiting, a blond beauty whose pink cheeks had been freshly kissed by the sun. Finally she nodded once. "Yes."

"Good. As soon as you get the doctor's approval, you can start." He turned to leave.

"I have a condition of my own."

He wheeled around, frustrated by the way she challenged him. "Which is?"

"When you disagree with my suggestions, and you will disagree," Susannah said, her smile kicking up the corners of her pretty lips, "will you at least try to understand that I'm making them for Darla's benefit?"

What did she think—that he was some bitter, angry, power monger who had to lord it over everyone to feel complete?

"I'll listen," David agreed, staring at her midriff. "As long as you promise you won't take any undue chances."

"With the baby?" Her face tightened. "No," she said firmly. "I want my baby to be healthy. I won't risk anything for that. That's one thing I don't intend to mess up."

"Then we have a deal."

David turned and walked away.

That's one thing I don't intend to mess up.

For the rest of the day, David couldn't stop speculating on Susannah's comment. What—or who—had let Susannah down, making her believe she had to earn love?

He found no satisfactory answers to stop his thoughts about Darla's newest caregiver—at least, that's how he *should* be thinking of the beautiful Susannah Wells.

Chapter Four

Two weeks later Susannah stirred under the November sun, stretched and blinked. The scene in front of her brought her wide awake.

"Do you like it?" Darla preened, scissors dangling from one finger.

"Um, it's different." Susannah slid her legs to one side and slowly rose. Thankfully her recent light-headedness seemed to have abated. She lifted the scissors from Darla's hands and put them on the patio table. "Let's put these away."

She'd slept a full eight hours last night. It wasn't as if she was tired. And yet, one minute of sun and she went out like a light. Sleeping on the job. David would be furious.

"Why did you cut off the bottom of your dress, sweetie?" Susannah asked.

"I don't like this dress," Darla grumbled. She flopped down into a chair. "Davy says it's nice but I think it's ugly."

"Because it's black?" Susannah asked. "But you look good in black. You have the right coloring."

Darla didn't look at her. Instead she drew her knees to her chin and peered into space.

"Why so serious?" Susannah laid a hand on the shiny dark head. "What are you thinking about, honey?"

"When my mom died, it was like today," Darla whispered. "There were leaves falling off the trees."

And you wore a black dress.

"Black isn't only for funerals, you know, Darla," she soothed. "Evening wear is often black because it looks so dressy. And a lot of women wear black to look slimmer."

"Am I fat?" Darla asked, eyes widening.

"No! Of course you're not. I didn't mean that." Susannah couldn't tell what was going on in the girl's mind, so she waited.

"Black clothes don't show marks when you spill stuff," the whisper came a minute later.

"Oh?" Something told Susannah to proceed very carefully.

"Davy and me went out for pizza last night. It was good, but I spilled."

"I'm sure the pizza people didn't care. Restaurants are used to spills," Susannah encouraged. "Besides, everyone gets messy eating pizza."

"Davy didn't. He had on a white shirt." Darla wouldn't look at her. "I wore my soccer shirt. It got stains. I looked like a baby."

Darla was worried about her appearance?

"Davy was embarr—" She frowned, unable to find the word.

"Embarrassed? I don't think David gets embarrassed." Susannah wasn't sure she completely understood what was behind these comments. But it was time to find out

why her clothes bothered Darla. She held out a hand.
"Come on."

"Where are we going?" Darla asked, taking Susannah's hand to help her rise.

"To look at your closet."

"Okay." Darla picked up the scissors.

"Without those," she added hastily.

"Oh." Darla put them back, then led the way to her room.

As they poked through the contents of the closet for the rest of the afternoon, Susannah watched Darla's reaction to each item. Mostly negative. Susannah had no idea how much time had passed when a sardonic voice in the doorway asked, "Did you lose something?"

"Oh. Hi." Darla had a point, Susannah decided. David looked as neat and pristine as he'd probably looked when he left the house this morning. She felt rumpled and dingy even being in the same room. "We're taking inventory."

"Ah." He blinked. "I'm going to change. You won't—er, leave the room like that, will you?"

"I think so." Susannah winked at Darla. "Has a certain carefree look, don't you think?"

But Darla didn't laugh. Instead she rose and began scooping up handfuls of hangers and placing them on the rod in her closet.

"I'll make it good, Davy," she said as she scurried back and forth.

"What happened to your dress?" he asked, staring at the ragged, sawed-off hem.

"Oh, that," Susannah said, noting Darla's flush of embarrassment. "I'm afraid that's a fashion plan gone wrong."

"You did it deliberately?" Pure shock robbed all expression from his face.

"It was unplanned," she hedged. "But the dress didn't work in its original state anyway."

"It worked for—never mind." His mouth drooped before he quickly closed it. He turned to leave, then stopped and turned back, dark eyes suspicious. "Did anything else happen today?"

"We did a little work in the back flower bed. Darla's really good at planting and we both like mums, so we planted a few pots."

"Then I owe you some money." He nodded. "If you'll meet me downstairs in a few minutes, I'll pay you."

"Good idea. I want to talk to you anyway." Susannah frowned. Was that fear flickering through his tawny eyes? Of her? "Five minutes?"

He nodded and left.

"Davy paid for my clothes. He likes them. So do I," Darla insisted loudly. She hurried to get the clothes hung, and in her haste the hangers dangled helter-skelter.

"Hey, slow down," Susannah chuckled. "I helped create this mess. I'm going to help you clean it up." By showing Darla how to group clothes, they reorganized the closet and rearranged the drawers. She paused when she pulled out an old pair of almost-white jeans tucked at the back of the closet. "How come you never wear these, Darla?"

"Davy doesn't like them. And I'm too big." Darla took them from her and relegated them to their hiding place. She took off the dress she'd cut and drew on another exactly the same except it was navy instead of black.

Clearly Darla didn't want to irritate the brother who had done so much for her. A lump of pity swelled in

Susannah's throat. Darla was willing to be unhappy rather than tell her brother she hated her clothes.

They walked downstairs together. Mrs. Peters, David's housekeeper, asked Darla to set the table just as he came loping down the stairs.

"Now how much do I owe you for the flowers?"

Susannah glanced down the hall, grabbed his elbow and drew him into his study. She closed the door.

"We have to make this quick before she finishes the table."

"Make what quick?" he asked, one eyebrow elegantly arched.

"Listen, I want to take Darla shopping," she explained.

"Shopping?" He nodded. "More flowers?"

"New clothes." She held up a hand. "You're going to say her clothes are almost new. I'm sure someone at the goodwill center will appreciate that."

"You cut her dress because you don't like her clothes," he guessed, a frown line marring the smooth perfection of his forehead. "Um—"

"Darla cut it. Because she hates it. And the rest of her clothes." Susannah flopped onto a couch and crossed her feet under her. "I can't say I blame her."

His chest puffed out. His face got that indignant look and his caramel eyes turned brittle. Susannah gulped. Okay, that could have been worded differently.

"What I mean is—"

"You mean her clothes aren't trendy. No holes in her jeans, no skintight shirts," he snapped. "Ms. Wells, my sister's clothes are from an expensive store. They are the best—"

"—money can buy," she finished. "I'm sure they are." She sat back and waited for him to cool down.

David continued to glare at her. Eventually he sat down and sighed. "Explain, please."

"Did you choose Darla's clothes? No, let me guess. You told a sales associate what you wanted and she picked them out." Susannah chuckled at the evidence radiating across his face. "I thought so. Probably a commissioned sales woman."

"What difference would that make?" he demanded. "I got the best for my sister. Darla doesn't need to alter her own clothes."

"She might be happier if she could tear them all apart," she mused.

"What? Where is this going?" He looked defensive and frustrated. That was not her goal. Susannah straightened, leaned forward.

"After she cut her dress, Darla told me she wore black the day of her mother's funeral. Then she talked a lot about spilling and messes." She inhaled a deep breath for courage. "Did you notice when you were in her room how many of her clothes are black, brown or gray?"

"Good serviceable colors," David said.

"For men's suits!" Susannah blew the straggling wisps of hair off her forehead and tried again. "Your sister is, what, three years younger than me? Can you imagine me in any of her clothes?"

"No."

Susannah surveyed her jeans. "I don't have good clothes, David. I bought most of mine at a thrift store. But you're right," she said flatly, "I wouldn't wear Darla's clothes if you gave them to me."

David glared at her. "Why don't you just come right out and say what you mean?"

"Did Darla choose any of those clothes?"

"I don't recall." He frowned, his gaze on some past

memory. "Her arm was still bothering her and she had some bandages yet to be removed when we shopped. We went for snaps and zips she could manage." Then he refocused. "Does it matter?"

"Yes!"

"Because?" He waited, shuffling one foot in front of the other.

"Because she should be young and carefree. Instead she wears the clothes of a forty-year-old," Susannah snapped, unable to hold in her irritation. "Because she needs to dress in something that lets her personality shine through. Because Darla is smothering under this blanket you keep putting over her."

"Well. Don't hold back." David stiffened, his face frozen.

"I wouldn't even if I could," she assured him. "I'm here to help Darla. That's what I'm trying to do."

"I'm not sure you fully understand Darla's situation," David said crisply. "Until about eight months ago, she could barely walk. She'd been wearing jogging suits while she did rehab. By the time she finished that, she'd outgrown everything she owned."

He'd done his best. That was the thing that kept Susannah from screaming at him to lighten up. No matter what, David Foster had done the very best he could for his sister. Because he loved her. Connie was right. He did have integrity. How could you fault that?

But Darla was her concern, not sparing David's feelings. Susannah leaned forward, intent on making him understand what she'd only begun to decipher.

"Darla is smart and funny. She's got a sweet heart and she loves people. But she doesn't have any confidence in herself." Susannah touched his arm. "She gets frustrated because she wants so badly to be what you want, and yet somehow, she just can't get there."

"I don't want her to be anything," he protested.

"You want her to be neat and tidy." Susannah pressed on, determined to make him see what she saw.

"That's wrong?" David asked.

"How many teens do you know who fit that designation? By nature teens are exploring, innovating, trying to figure out their world. Darla is no different." Susannah said. "Except that she thinks you're embarrassed when she spills something."

"I'm not embarrassed about anything to do with my sister." She saw the truth in his frank stare. "I thought…"

The complete uncertainty washing over his face gripped a soft spot in her heart.

"David, listen to me and, just for a moment, pretend that I know what I'm talking about." She drew in a breath of courage. "Most teen girls love fashion, they love color. They experiment with style, trying to achieve the looks they see in magazines. It's part of figuring out who they are. I'll bet Darla used to do that, didn't she?"

"She always liked red," he said slowly.

"I didn't see anything red in her closet."

"No." His solemn voice said he'd absorbed what she'd hinted at. "Go on."

"With her current wardrobe, Darla couldn't experiment if she wanted to," Susannah told him. "Her clothes are like a mute button on a TV. They squash everything unique and wonderful about her."

"But—" David stopped, closed his mouth and stared at her.

His silence encouraged Susannah to continue, though she softened her tone.

"I think her accident left her trying to figure out how she fits into her new world. She's struggling to make what she is inside match with those boring clothes."

"So how should she dress?" he asked, his eyes on her worn jeans.

"I want her to express herself. If she's in a happy mood, I want her to be able to pull on something bright and cheerful. If she's feeling down, I want her to express that, instead of becoming so frustrated she blows out of control and tantrums."

A timid knock interrupted.

"Are you mad at me for cutting my dress, Davy?" Darla peeked around the door, her big brown eyes soulful as a puppy's. "I'm sorry."

"It's okay, Dar. It was just a dress." David patted the seat beside him. "Come here for a minute, will you?"

Susannah wanted to cry as the tall, beautiful girl shuffled across the room, shoulders down, misery written all over her demeanor when she flopped down beside her brother.

"Ms. Wells has been telling me she thinks you need some new clothes."

"Really?" Darla jerked upright, her face brightening.

"Would you like to go shopping?" he asked.

For a moment hope glittered in Darla's dark eyes but it fizzled out when she shook her head.

"No. I have lots of clothes. I hung them all up, Davy."

"I know you did, honey. That's great." He smoothed her hair back. "You know, Dar, when we got those clothes you were still getting better from your accident and you had trouble with zippers and buttons." He laid an arm around her shoulders and hugged her. "But you're much better now. I think we should get you some new things, especially with Thanksgiving and Christmas coming. What do you think?"

"Connie's going to have a party. I could get a new dress for that." Darla's face cleared and she grinned. "Okay, Davy."

Susannah wanted to cheer. He'd phrased it just right. Everyone got new clothes for the holidays. It was a natural decision, revealing no reflection on the ugly things now in Darla's wardrobe. Little by little they could be shifted out.

"Can Susannah get a party dress, too?"

Susannah blinked, then shook her head. "Oh, no, I don't—"

"Why not?" David smiled at Darla.

"I don't want a new dress," Susannah protested. "With the baby, that is—" She blushed and avoided his stare. "I won't fit in anything for very long and—"

"There are such things as maternity dresses," he said mildly. "Besides, you'll need something for Connie's Christmas party. It's quite a fancy affair. Tomorrow's Saturday. That's a good day for shopping. I'll pay you overtime."

"No, you won't." Distressed by the way this had turned on her, Susannah rose. "I'm sure the two of you will manage very well tomorrow."

"Oh, no. You're not sticking me with a shopping trip on my own. We'll pick you up at ten. Right, Darla?" He grinned at his sister, who grinned right back.

"Right. I'm going to tell Mrs. Peters." She rushed away, all arms and legs and excitement, exactly as a teenage girl would.

Susannah stared after her, amazed by the change. When she felt David watching her, she looked away from the intensity of his gaze and walked toward the front door.

"We could start at Bayley's Store for Women," he said, following her.

Her hand on the doorknob, Susannah froze. She turned and looked at him.

"For more of the same?" she asked.

"Point made." He sighed. "Okay, you can pick the stores. But nothing too…"

Susannah couldn't help but roll her eyes. "David, could you just lighten up? Try to remember what it was like when you were her age. It wasn't that long ago," she teased gently.

She thought she saw humor in those toffee-toned eyes, but before she could be sure, David blinked.

"Ten o'clock, remember. How much did you spend on the flowers?" He pulled out his wallet and handed her some money. "Will this cover it?"

"It's too much." Susannah held out her hand, offering it back. But David shook his head.

"No, it isn't. I'm pretty sure you stopped somewhere along the way for a drink, didn't you? And something to eat?"

"How do you know that?" she asked. He grinned, his smile dazzling her. She was momentarily stunned by how great he looked when he smiled.

"Because I'm getting to know you." He reached out and touched the corner of her mouth. "And because you have a little smear of chocolate right here."

"Oh." Her stomach shivered and it had nothing to do with the baby or morning sickness. "Right. Well, I guess I'll see you tomorrow," she said. "Bye."

Susannah turned and literally fled from the man

whose touch had just sent warmth flooding through her. Her skin burned where he'd brushed his fingers.

She'd thought David stern and taciturn, but he'd surprised her. Maybe under all that lawyerly reserve and rule making, David Foster wasn't quite the ogre she'd thought.

David shifted uncomfortably on the dinky little chair someone had thought to provide for men stuck waiting while women tried on clothes. He'd like to leave, but he wanted to vet every outfit his sister tried on. So far, his decisions had not been popular with Susannah, who, by the way, seemed perfectly at home on her little perch.

"Uh, I don't think so," he said, when Darla emerged in a swirling lime-green tank top and matching pants.

"Oh, why not?" Susannah asked. "Too much color?"

"No. The pants don't fit her properly. They're too short." He didn't understand the droll look Darla and Susannah exchanged.

"It's a capri pant," Susannah explained. "They're supposed to be that length. It's the fashion."

"Oh." Fashion. He felt like he was drowning.

"So?" Susannah nudged him with her elbow.

"Do you like it?" he asked his sister, studying her face.

"Yes." At least she was definite. "Emmaline wears clothes like this at my school. She's pretty."

"You look pretty, too," he told her. And she did.

Contrary to David's expectations, Susannah's choices for his sister were not outlandish or edgy. Nor were they as expensive as the clothes he'd chosen. He was amazed at Susannah's patience as she taught Darla to choose the things that brought out her natural beauty. With each outfit, as Darla caught a glimpse of herself in the mirror, she grew more graceful. More and more she was becoming the sister he remembered, leaving behind the mulish child he'd battled with for the last eight months.

It wouldn't last, of course. Darla had a long way to go. But she was learning, and Susannah had lasted much longer than any of Darla's other caregivers.

"You should be proud. She's a very beautiful woman," Susannah murmured.

Woman? His sister?

David did a double take at the girl in the red dress now preening in the mirror. But Susannah was right. Darla looked more like a young woman than a girl. She was growing up and he'd have to face all that implied.

"I want Susannah to try on this dress." Darla held out a garment of swirling patterns in deep, rich green. "It has room for the baby," she said.

"It's very beautiful, Darla, and I appreciate you thinking of me," Susannah said quietly. "But I can't try it on. It's too expensive."

"I want you to. It's a present." Darla the woman disappeared, and the petulant girl returned, face turning red when Susannah continued to shake her head. "Davy, buy it," she insisted, thrusting the hanger at her brother.

"Darla, I can't accept it." Susannah was firm but insistent. "Please put it back on the rack."

"No. It's your dress." Darla was working herself up into a snit.

David rose, preparing to leave.

"Sit down please, David. We're not finished yet." Susannah never even looked at him, but her firm tone and calm manner left him in no doubt as to who was in charge.

David sat.

"Put the dress back, please, Darla. Then we need to look at shoes." Susannah blandly continued to survey the list in her hand.

Darla was still angry but now she looked confused.

"I want you to have a new dress, too," she said, her voice quieter as she stood in front of Susannah.

"I know you do, sweetie. And it's very kind of you, but this shopping day is for you. When I decide to get a new dress, I promise you and I will go shopping for it. But not today." She paused, studied the girl. "Okay?"

Darla's internal battle was written all over her face. But Susannah's calm tone and manner won. Darla returned the dress to the rack, changed back into her own clothes and calmly waited while the sales clerk totaled her purchases.

David handed over his credit card in total bemusement. How did Susannah do it?

"Can we have lunch before we start shoe shopping?" he asked as they stored the many packages in his vehicle. "I'm starving."

"That's because you didn't eat a good breakfast. Breakfast is the most important meal of the day. More than half of North Americans skip breakfast." Darla told him, stuffing her last package into the trunk.

"Half?" Susannah sputtered.

David looked at her. She was trying to hide her laughter.

"Yes, half," Darla insisted.

"Then I guess I'm one of those statistics," Susannah told her. "I'm starving, too. And your stomach is growling." She giggled out loud and soon Darla was giggling with her.

Shaking his head, David led them to a restaurant and left Susannah to deal with Darla's insistence on chocolate cake while he scoured the menu for himself. He'd forgotten how nice it was to relax over a meal.

Susannah didn't insist Darla choose anything, he discovered. She commented on the results of certain choices, and then left the decision totally up to Darla, who glanced at him for approval.

"You decide," David said quietly.

And she did, visibly gaining confidence as she discarded the chocolate cake in favor of another choice.

"I don't like soup," she told the server. "It's messy. Can I have something else?"

They settled on a salad to go with her cheeseburger and fries. Usually David ordered something she could munch on right away, but Darla seemed perfectly content to talk as they waited for their food. After a moment she excused herself and went to wash her hands.

"How do you do it?" David asked Susannah the moment his sister was out of hearing range. "She hasn't tantrumed with you once, though I thought we'd have one in the store."

"I did, too," Susannah confessed with a grin. "And if she had, I would have sat there and waited it out."

"Really?" He couldn't imagine sitting through one of Darla's tantrums.

"It's a behavior she's learned, David. She needs time to unlearn it." She shrugged. "If we make her responsible for her actions, she'll soon realize that the results she gets are determined by her. I want her to learn independence."

"We had a big argument about her bedtime last night," he admitted. "She thinks she should stay up longer. Maybe she should," he admitted. "I guess I still think of her as a little kid."

"She is in some ways." Susannah sipped her lemonade.

"Why don't you let her choose a time on the condition that she has to get up in the morning when her alarm clock rings without your help? Make her responsible."

"Good idea." He sipped his coffee. "I can't believe you learned all this caring for the elderly."

"Some of it," she admitted. "But most of what I know about behavior, I learned in our foster home. And I took some university classes for a semester. They helped. I'm going to take some more. I want to get a degree in psychology."

He was intrigued by her. More than a boss should be.

"The bathroom is really pretty," Darla told them as she slipped back into her seat. "Lots of red."

Their food arrived and conversation became sporadic. David dug into his steak, then paused to notice that Susannah picked certain items off her plate and set them aside but eagerly bit into a sour pickle.

"So it's true what they say about pregnancies and pickles," he teased.

She flushed a rich ruby flood of color that tinted her skin from the V neckline of her sweater to the roots of her hair. Finally she nodded.

"It's true. For me anyway."

"I don't like pickles," Darla said. "You can have mine, Susannah."

"Thank you." Susannah laid the pickles on one slice of toast, then spread peanut butter on the other. She put them together, cut the whole thing in half and then took a bite.

"That's lunch?"

She blushed again when she caught him staring at her. "It's very good. You should try it."

"I'll take your word for it." Then it dawned on him. "Some foods bother you."

"Mostly the smell of some foods," she murmured, eyeing his steak with her nose turned up. She returned to munching contentedly on her sandwich.

"Connie said you'd seen the doctor I researched. She says everything is okay." It sounded like he was prying, he realized—which he was.

"I'm fine," she said. She set down her sandwich and stared at him. "The baby is fine. I'm very healthy. There's nothing to worry about."

"There's always something to worry about," he muttered, pushing away his plate.

"Why?" Susannah dabbed absently at a dribble of pickle juice and waited for an answer. "I thought Connie told me you believe in God."

"I do."

"People who believe in God usually talk about the faith they have in Him to lead them," she mused, perking up when a dessert cart arrived at the table next to theirs. "What are you worried about?"

"A new study says ninety percent of the things people worry about will never happen," Darla chimed in.

Susannah tucked her chin against her neck but not fast enough to hide her grin. David was beginning to wish he'd never said a word about worry, so he grabbed at their server's suggestions for dessert and bought everyone a huge piece of key lime pie. With the meal finished, he begged off shoe shopping and agreed to meet the two women in a little courtyard area outside. Better to trust Susannah than sit through another round of fashion dos and don'ts.

He was enjoying a well-creamed cup of coffee and working out a schedule of Darla's activities on his

BlackBerry when Susannah arrived lugging several bags, visibly weary. He took them from her and insisted she sit down.

"Where's Darla?" he asked, searching the area behind her.

"She's coming. She met a friend and they're buying an ice cream cone. Her friend's mother will meet us here shortly." Susannah chose a seat in a shady spot where she could study the dangling seed pods of a desert willow. "You were working," she said. "Don't let me bother you."

"No bother." He stuffed the device in his pocket. "I just got an email about Darla's after-school soccer group. I guess I forgot to reregister her."

"Does she have to go?" Susannah asked.

"She loves soccer." He frowned. "Doesn't she?"

"Yes." Susannah didn't meet his stare. "But there are so many more things she wants to try."

"Such as?" He could feel the tension crawling across his shoulders. What was wrong with the status quo? Why did she have to change everything?

"Did you know she wants to do pottery again?"

"I know she liked it before. But it's not very active and Darla needs to keep her muscles toned. Soccer is good for that," he explained.

"Swimming is better."

David tensed. Why was she always so eager to push him?

"I'm not comfortable with her swimming. At least not without me present," he said, waving when Darla emerged from the store. "For now I think we'll stick to the activities she knows."

"The ones you've decided are safe for her, right?"

Susannah smiled at Darla but her tone was troubled. "I hope you don't regret it," she said quietly.

David was going to ask what she meant but Darla snagged his attention, showing him the massive cone she was trying to eat before it melted. She giggled and laughed, teased Susannah about the pickle juice that had spattered her shirt and insisted David taste her triple-fudge-and-marshmallow ice cream.

David discarded Susannah's comment. Darla was happy, like a big kid enjoying the pleasures of life. That was exactly what he wanted for her.

Wasn't it?

Unbidden, the image of Darla twirling in front of the store's floor-length mirror in her red dress fluttered through his mind. Not a kid, a woman. He felt the intensity of a stare and caught Susannah looking at him.

She was good for his sister. He didn't deny that. But there were things in Darla's life that *were* working, things that didn't need changing. One of those was soccer.

He urged them back to the car and drove Susannah to Connie's, anxious to escape her probing questions and retreat to the normalcy of his home.

But that night, when the house had quieted and there was no one to disturb his thoughts, David couldn't dislodge Susannah's warning from his brain.

I hope you don't regret it.

"Maybe I'm not supposed to worry about things, Lord," he whispered as he sat in the dark, watching stars diamond-stud the black velvet of the night sky. "But I am worried. She's changing everything. What if Susannah's wrong about Darla?"

But what if she was right?

Chapter Five

This is wrong.

It wasn't the first time Susannah had thought those words as she stood in the church basement and watched Darla try to interact with the young girls in the club.

It wasn't that they were mean or did anything to Darla. In fact, they were most impressed with Darla's new outfit and offered many compliments.

The problem was Darla didn't fit here and she knew it. The other girls were younger, faster and more nimble with their handicrafts. Darla tried, but only halfheart-edly, and when her kite didn't work out, she crushed it and threw it into the trash in a fit of anger.

Susannah saw the glint in her eye and the set of her jaw and knew the girl was not happy. The ride home was tense. On an impulse she pulled into a park.

"Let's go for a walk," she said.

After they'd gone a short way, Darla stopped.

"I hate girls' club. I can't do it." She stamped her foot, caught Susannah's eye and sighed. "I'm sorry," she said, flopping onto the grass.

"Actually, I think you did very well at girls' club, but maybe you've been there long enough," Susannah mused, sitting beside her. Maybe here Darla would open up and speak of things she did want to do.

"Davy likes girls' club. He says it's safe."

"I suppose it is safe," Susannah said, striving to sound noncommittal.

"It's for little kids. I'm not little." After a few minutes Darla began talking about the bed of flowers nearby. She described each one.

"You know a lot about flowers." Susannah's mind had begun to whirl with ideas but she gave nothing away. She'd have to talk to David first, get his permission. And that would probably not be easy.

"I like them. Flowers don't make me feel stupid," Darla muttered. Then her face brightened. "There's the ice cream man. I love ice cream. Maybe they have pistachio. Can I get one, Susannah?" Darla begged.

"I don't know if I have enough cash. Maybe you should find out how much a cone costs first?" Susannah stayed where she was, swamped by a rush of tiredness as Darla raced across the grass.

In a few minutes Darla came rushing back. Susannah held out her wallet and Darla counted out what she needed. It seemed a lot to Susannah. She'd been trying to save every cent she could for the baby but these little side trips were digging into that meager account.

Still, it was worth it to see Darla's proud face as she returned with two fudge bars.

"One for you and one for me."

"Thank you." Susannah took the bar, impressed again by Darla's kind heart. "That's very kind of you to share. Didn't they have pistachio?"

"I'd rather have a fudge one with you," Darla said.

She'd given up her first choice to share. Susannah felt proud as any new mom.

While they ate their cones, Darla talked about her brother.

"Davy's an awfully good brother," she said, her eyes soft with love. "He was on a vacation when my dad died. Davy had to come home and take over his work. When my mom got sick, Davy looked after her, too." Her smile dimmed. "And he always looks after me."

"He loves you a lot."

"I love him, too," Darla said. "I wish he would have gotten married. But Erin didn't want me around." Darla peeked sideways at Susannah, her guilt obvious.

"What happened?" She kept her voice even.

"I wasn't nice. I spilled ketchup on her shirt. Her favorite shirt." A glower replaced Darla's sunny smile. "She told Davy I was a baby, too young to make pots."

"Pots? Oh, you mean pottery?" She shrugged. "Maybe you were too young, honey. I'm afraid I don't know anything about it."

"I do. A man came to my school and showed us how to make pots. He said mine was the best," she said proudly. "Davy put it in the garden."

"You mean the blue one?" Susannah asked, surprised by the information.

"Uh-huh. It was going to be a fountain but it dried too hard and I couldn't put a hole in it." She sighed. "The teacher told me I should try again."

"Maybe you should."

"You mean it, Susannah? You'll let me do pottery?" Darla leaned over and hugged her tightly. "Oh, thank you."

Susannah ignored the blob of chocolate on her shirt-front and hugged back. "It isn't up to me, so don't get in a rush. I have to ask your brother. He's the boss and if he says no—"

She left it hanging. Finished with the ice cream, they rinsed off under a tap and then drove home. Darla immediately stormed David with a demand to make pottery.

As Susannah watched them, she grew very conscious of the way he surveyed her, his gaze resting on the twin ice cream stains the two of them wore. Well, so what? They'd had fun.

His mouth pursed in that thin line that meant he was going to deny Darla's request out of hand. Susannah had to do something.

"Darla, would you show me the pot you made? I'd really like to see it again." She followed the young woman to the back garden to admire the shiny blue pot that held a barrel cactus. "It would have made a lovely fountain," she agreed.

After much discussion about pottery, Mrs. Peters came to ask Darla's help. Darla left, and David turned to her. Susannah stiffened, knowing what was coming.

"Why this sudden need for pottery?" David asked. He pointed to a chair. "Please sit down. You look worn out."

Just what every woman wanted to hear.

"It's not *my* need, it's Darla's," she said, folding into the comfortable garden chair with relief. "She didn't have the best time at clubs—again."

"What happened," he demanded. "What did she do?"

"Darla didn't *do* anything," Susannah told him. "But she's too big for that club and she knows it. It doesn't interest her." She straightened and told him in a rush, "I don't think she should go anymore."

"What?" He glared at her. "Why not?"

"David, Darla can do so much more than play with little girls. She's lost some faculties, but she still has lots of skills and interests. Plants, for instance," she said, cutting off the question she knew was coming.

"I suppose I could clear out some of the things my mother planted," he said, studying the lovely garden.

"You could, but she needs more than that." Susannah struggled to explain what she'd begun to understand about Darla. "What would you do if you didn't have your work, David?" she asked.

"Me?" He shrugged. "I always wanted to fly. I have my private license. Why?"

"You have options. Darla is trying to figure out what hers are," Susannah told him. "She wants to do something that makes her feel good about herself, something that shows for her efforts, and maybe something that helps others. She needs to feel confident about herself first, though."

"I don't think pottery is an option right now," he mused. "I don't think there are any classes going that she could attend. What else do you have in mind to help her learn this confidence?"

"Swimming." She shook her head at him. "I know *you're* afraid for her, but I think she's ready to challenge herself. She's ashamed that she can't go with her class when they go for swimming lessons. She knows she's missing out, David. Think how much self-esteem she'd have if she went with the class and had no problem in the water."

She knew he understood. He was clever and thoughtful and he wanted Darla to be happy. But something was holding him back.

"What if she panics?" he demanded in a tense voice.

"What if she does? They have trained staff who deal with that all the time. Darla isn't the first one to be afraid of water." Susannah touched his hand. "I know you want to keep her safe. And she will be. But she needs personal and physical challenges to grow and develop."

"But swimming?" He drew back from her touch, his face shadowed by the awning above.

A thought crossed Susannah's mind. "Do you swim, David?"

"Why do you ask?" He looked at her then, straight and head on.

"I ask because it seems like you're projecting your fears onto Darla. And I know that isn't what you want to do." She waited a few moments, watching the truth fill his face. "What happened?" she murmured.

"Are you psychoanalyzing me, Ms. Wells?"

"Do you have something to hide, Mr. Foster?"

It took several moments before he let out a deep breath.

"I was twenty-five. Old enough I suppose, but I never expected—" He shook his head. "My mother was a swimmer. We used to have a pool back here. She loved that pool, did laps every day. I came home one afternoon and found her floating on the water. She'd had a stroke."

"I'm so sorry." He was in his own world now, tied up in a knot of guilt. Susannah tried to nudge him out. "Did she recover?"

"Not really. She was paralyzed till she died. She never swam again."

"But that wasn't your fault." Something in his face didn't compute. "David?"

"I was so scared," he blurted. "I did all the wrong things. It took forever to get her out of the water because I was afraid of hurting her. I should have done more resuscitation but when she didn't come to, I panicked."

He stared at her. "If it hadn't been for my friend Jared showing up, she would have died."

"So you had the pool filled in and you've been blaming yourself and trying desperately to stop anything like that from happening to Darla." Susannah smiled sadly. "But you're drowning her with your rules and regulations, David."

He held her gaze, not looking away even when Darla returned.

"It's late. I'd better go." Susannah rose slowly, forcing herself not to give away the fact that the yard was spinning.

"Can Susannah stay for dinner, Davy?" Darla asked.

"Not tonight, thanks," Susannah said before he could refuse. "I think I'm going to go home and lie down."

"Shall I drive you?" David's face was drawn and serious.

"Don't be silly. It's just a couple of blocks." She headed for the front door.

"All the same, you look pale. I think you should ride." He told Darla to stay with Mrs. Peters, then took Susannah's elbow and escorted her to his car.

"This is silly. I'm fine," she protested, but he ignored her.

"You're overdoing it. That was not my intent when you took this job. Maybe you should cut back. I can find someone else to work with Darla." He backed out of his driveway and pulled onto the street.

"Look, the doctor assures me that part of pregnancy is the occasional tiredness. I'm really fine." She saw him glance at her stomach and pulled down her shirt defensively. "I'm not some delicate flower. I'm tough, resilient." She breathed a mocking laugh. "I survived Nick. I can handle having a baby."

"Nick's the guy who left you?" he asked as he pulled up in front of Connie's house.

"He was the man I thought I married." Shame washed over her. "I stupidly thought he loved me."

"Why stupidly?" David turned in his seat to face her. "Why wouldn't he love you?"

"Because I'm a total failure," she told him, trying to suppress the tears. "People like me aren't the type who get happily ever after. I'm not like Connie. She took her life and made something of it. I messed up."

Susannah was too ashamed to sit there and let him see her give way to tears so she hastily exited the car.

"Thanks for the ride. Good night."

She hurried away, listening for the sound of the car leaving. But in her room, when she glanced out of the window, she saw him still sitting there, a puzzled look on his face.

A long time passed before he finally left.

"And now it's finally clear to him what a twit I am." Susannah sighed and started a bath. Some days were better forgotten. This was definitely one of them.

She caught a glimpse of herself in the mirror just before she stepped into the tub.

"Your mother is an idiot," she whispered, allowing the tears to fall unheeded. "Not the kind of mommy you deserve at all."

"Darla, did Susannah seem okay today?" David pretended nonchalance as he waited for his sister's response later that evening.

"I dunno." Darla looked up. "She gets tired sometimes. I pretend I am, too, so she can rest."

"That's nice of you. What did you do today?" He

listened as Darla recited their activities. "That doesn't seem too bad."

"No. But I don't think Susannah has much money. When we were in the park, I wanted an ice cream cone, but when she opened her wallet, I saw that she only had enough money for me to have a cone. So I got two little bars instead. One for each of us."

"I'm proud of you for thinking of that." David's chest swelled.

"Yeah." She grinned at him.

"Maybe she doesn't carry much money with her," he mused.

"She always puts some of her money in a little can at Connie's. It's her baby can. She's saving." Darla grabbed the remote. "Can I watch my TV program now?"

"Sure."

Susannah didn't have much money. Well, of course she didn't. He'd forgotten to give her money for gas. Darla's old hot rod would bankrupt Midas.

Come to think of it, Susannah wouldn't have an easy time with those bucket seats a few months down the road, either. Maybe it was time to trade it in. The car had been secondhand when he'd got it for Darla, just before her skiing accident. It still ran, but he didn't like the idea of Susannah possibly getting stopped somewhere.

You're worried about her safety now? The chiding voice in the back of his head mocked.

David returned to the television room, oblivious to Darla's program. He wanted to shut that voice down, but the memory of Susannah's face when he'd driven her home, the pain in her voice as she'd spoken about the louse who dumped her, the thought of her innocent child caught in the midst of it all—well, David couldn't get rid of those thoughts.

"Davy?" Darla shut off the television. "Can I talk to you?"

"Of course. You can always talk to me." He patted the sofa and waited for her to curl up beside him. "What's up?"

"I was wondering who will be the daddy for Susannah's baby."

"Umm, what makes you ask, honey?" he sidestepped.

"Well, today I saw her watching a little boy when we were in the park. What if her baby is a boy? Boys need daddies to play with them and teach them stuff that mommies can't." Darla's nose scrunched up as she mulled over the problem.

"Well, maybe the father will come when the baby's born."

But Darla shook her head.

"Nope. His name was Nick and he died. I heard Aunt Connie telling Uncle Wade. He was a scoun—" She squeezed her eyes closed, trying to recall the word, but finally gave up. "I can't remember," she finally admitted.

The baby's father was dead—meaning there was no chance for Susannah to get support from him, financially or otherwise. And he *was* a scoundrel, David thought as his back teeth clenched.

You're not getting involved. You don't need any more responsibilities.

"*Scoundrel*. I think he was a bad man," Darla continued. "Don't you?"

"I don't know." He shouldn't even be listening to this, but David was curious. More curious than he should have been.

"I don't think a nice man would tell Susannah to get

out. That's mean." Darla snuggled up to him. "She let me touch her tummy where the baby is growing."

"Oh." David smoothed her hair. Was it wrong to talk about this? He found himself eager to hear every detail about the beautiful blonde and her child. Maybe because he felt he'd never have his own child.

"Susannah said she doesn't know anything about how to be a mommy," Darla said. "But I think she'll be a good mother. She's really nice to me, even when I'm not nice."

"I think Susannah's nice, too, Dar." Wasn't that an understatement.

He kissed the top of her head, surprised when she jumped up. "Hey, where are you going?"

"To make some popcorn. I'm hungry." She scurried away in her jeans and bright red shirt, her bare feet slapping against the hardwood.

David could count on one hand the evenings they'd shared like this before Susannah. Evenings were usually a battle zone, but since Connie's friend had shown up Darla was more like her old self. Susannah was doing amazing work.

His mind suddenly replayed what Darla had told him.

So this Nick had told Susannah to get out? Knowing she was pregnant?

No wonder she sometimes seemed like a glass ornament, brittle and ready to shatter. Her tough veneer was just a facade, perhaps to shield herself from being hurt again. Connie had hinted at something in her past. Something ugly.

But David wasn't going to get involved.

Keep telling yourself that.

He had to. Though David felt a rush of relief that no

bitter, angry boyfriend or husband was likely to come after Susannah, though he was glad that she and Darla would be safe from that, and though he was also grateful for the progress she was making with his sister—well, the rest of it was her life.

And none of his business.

"What are you thinking about, Davy?" Darla flopped at his feet, her cheeks bulging with popcorn.

He snatched one of the fluffy white bits and popped it into his mouth.

"I'm thinking about buying a different car for you and Susannah to use."

"Good. Susannah will be glad, too," Darla told him. "She says the seat hurts her back. And she has to sit on a cushion to see."

The things you could learn if you only paid attention.

"Davy?"

"Yeah?"

"Could you think about something else now?" Darla said, her brown eyes on him, sizing him up.

"What's that?" He was half-afraid to ask.

"I don't want to go to girls' club anymore. I'm too big." She thrust her feet in front of her and stared at her poppy-red toenails.

"Okay. I'll tell them you won't be coming." He waited, knowing Darla was forming another thought.

"Do you think I'm too dumb to swim, Davy?"

He might have known.

"What do you think?"

"I don't know. At first I was scared to try, but Susannah says new things often scare us but that doesn't mean we shouldn't try them." Darla stared at him quizzically.

"Do you think I can learn to not be afraid in the water, Davy?" The yearning in her voice was his undoing.

"I think you're very smart. I think that if you try hard, listen to the teacher and don't get frustrated, you can do a whole lot of things you never thought you could do," he said with certainty.

"I think maybe I can, too," she whispered. And then she grinned at him and held up her hand for a high five.

"I'll check on lessons tomorrow," he promised.

"Good. Because I don't like watching when my class goes swimming." Suddenly her eyes danced with excitement. "I'm going to surprise them when I swim right to the other end of the big pool!"

David could hardly believe the transformation in his sister.

What a difference Susannah Wells had made in their lives.

David wasn't going to get involved in her life, but that didn't have to stop him from praying that God would help her.

Her and her baby.

The beginning of a family.

He shut down that thought. A family was the one thing he couldn't have. He knew that wasn't God's plan for his life and had accepted it.

No point in dwelling on the impossible.

Chapter Six

"There are tons of flowers," Darla burbled, her voice rising. "And you know what else they had at the botanical garden?"

"No. What?"

On Friday afternoon Susannah drove the almost-new station wagon away from the school with a light heart. It was so much easier to handle than David's other car. She had no idea what had prompted him to change vehicles, but she was glad of it.

"There's a butterfly room. It's a special glass room with plants and fish and stuff, and butterflies live there. They came and sat on me!" Darla rushed on, enthusiastic about her latest school trip.

Susannah let her talk as they drove home, knowing that she needed to spill all the things that were tumbling around in her head. They were still bubbling over when David arrived.

"Can we go back tomorrow, Davy? I want to show you the butterflies."

"I'm sorry, Dar, I can't. Tomorrow's my day for my boys." He turned to Susannah. "Actually I was going to ask you if you could come tomorrow. I'm big brother to three boys and we do something special once a month. Tomorrow it's a hockey game in Phoenix. I just got the tickets."

Big brother? David? Surprise kept her silent.

"Darla doesn't like hockey so she doesn't want to come. Do you have other plans, Susannah?" he asked.

He was always so polite, yet somehow distant. As if he didn't want to get too involved in her world. Not that Susannah blamed him. Her world was messed up.

"Susannah?" Darla poked her in the arm. "Are you sick?"

"No." She smiled to ease Darla's worried expression. "I was just thinking that I'd like to see your botanical gardens tomorrow. I should see some of the sights while I'm here."

"Are you thinking of leaving Tucson?" David suddenly seemed to stumble over his words. "Not that you owe me any answers. But I would like a bit of notice to find someone else to stay with Darla."

"I don't want you to go away, Susannah." Darla's face darkened. Her hands fisted at her sides and her body stiffened. "You can't go."

"I never said I was going anywhere right now," Susannah reminded quietly. "But if I had to leave, I hope you would wish me the best."

Darla thought about it for several moments. Finally the anger drained away and her sunny smile flashed again.

"I would," she agreed, winding her arm around Susannah's waist. She leaned her head on her shoulder. "You're my best friend, and I like doing things with you. Please stay." She glanced over one shoulder at David before she leaned near to whisper, "I want to see your baby when it's born."

Susannah flushed. David would not want to hear that. He might be glad she was here to watch Darla, but Susannah didn't need him to say out loud how much he disapproved of her. It was evident in the distant way he acted.

"The baby won't be here for a long time," Susannah murmured, with a quick peek at his face. It was hard to read anything in those inscrutable eyes. "So how about I go with you tomorrow and see those butterflies? They sound fun."

"They are." Darla once more launched into a description that lasted until Mrs. Peters came to say good-night and reminded them of the potluck supper at church.

"I forgot all about that supper. Go change, Dar." David waited until she ran up the stairs, then beckoned to Susannah to follow him to the kitchen. "I've wanted to hear tonight's speaker for a long time. He worked on a mission in the Amazon."

"You know the Amazon?"

"I took a trip there with Wade and Jared just after we all finished college." He smiled. A certain wistfulness tinged his voice. "It was amazing. Unfortunately we had to leave early."

Was that when his father had died? She hated to ask and bring up painful memories.

"You never went back?" she asked.

"Haven't had time so far." He pulled an envelope out of a drawer and handed it to her. "This is yours."

"What's this?" she asked, confused when she saw the money tucked inside. "You already paid me for the last two weeks."

"Wages, yes. That's for incidentals. Like gas for the car, the botanical garden tomorrow and the numerous ice creams and other treats my sister seems to inhale. I never expected you to pay for them, Susannah. I just didn't think about it until Darla reminded me." He glanced once at her midsection. "I'm sure you're trying to save—for the baby, I mean."

"I am, but it doesn't seem right to take this." Susannah set the envelope on the table. "You already pay me very well for doing almost nothing."

"Nothing?" He said with incredulity. "It's a lot more than nothing to me. It's been ages since I've been so caught up at work."

"Oh, good." She blushed under his praise.

"It means a great deal to me to know Darla's safe and happy under your care, Susannah. And she's learning, too. Take it. Please." He handed her the envelope again. "You'll get the same every week. And if you need more for some activity, please tell me."

"Well—thank you." She tucked it into her bag while mentally calculating how much more she'd need to save before she could get the sonogram the doctor had recommended.

An awkward silence yawned.

"Are you feeling all right? She's not too much for you?" David asked in a careful voice.

"I'm fine. Darla's wonderful. She goes out of her way to watch out for me," Susannah told him. "She's always bringing me a cushion or a glass of water. She fusses too much. She shouldn't waste her attention on me."

He'd been packing items into a cooler, but he stopped and turned to study her, his brow furrowed.

"Waste?" He shook his head. "Darla loves you."

"She shouldn't."

"Why?" His eyes were wide with surprise.

"You wouldn't understand," she murmured, trying to think up some way to get out of this conversation.

"Because you think I've had the perfect life?" His dark eyes flashed with intensity. "I'm a spoiled rich kid because I never went through foster care like you and Connie?"

"No." She did meet his stare. "I don't believe anyone has a perfect life. No one I know anyway."

"Then?" He stood where he was, waiting, palms up, for some answer.

"Look, you had your life mapped out in front of you and you followed that map." It frustrated her to have to put into words what hurt so deeply. "You weren't like me. You didn't mess up over and over. Your choices were smart. Mine weren't."

"But you were a kid and that was ages ago," he said. "You've changed."

"Have I? I hope so. But the results of my stupid decisions live on," she said, laying a hand over her stomach as if she could protect her baby. "They're certainly not the decisions a mother wants to tell her child."

"Susannah, that's ridiculous. Everyone makes mistakes—"

"You didn't," she said, daring him to contradict.

"I'm ready." Darla stood in the doorway, her smile fading. "Are you arguing?" she asked, her voice worried.

"No. Just discussing." David touched her nose. "You look very pretty," he complimented.

"It's the same color as Susannah's shirt," she said proudly. "We both like pink."

Susannah's heart lifted, as it always did in the presence of this lovely girl. "Connie made this shirt. She's decided she is going to sew me a whole new wardrobe and she won't take no for an answer."

"Connie's like Davy." Darla peeked through her lashes at her big brother. "He doesn't take no, either."

"Hey! No dissing me." He smiled at Susannah. "You look very nice."

"Thank you." She fought to keep from blushing again, but that didn't stop her heart from bouncing with pleasure at the compliment. How stupid was that—to be glad a man who looked down on you thought you looked nice? Pregnancy was fooling with her brain.

"Darla, why don't you go put on your coat?" David said. When she'd left, he turned to Susannah. "Would you like to come to the potluck with us?" he asked as he closed the lid on the cooler. "I'm sure the presentation will be worth seeing."

"Go with you?" Susannah didn't understand for a moment. "Oh, you mean to watch her? Sure, I—"

"No, that's okay—Darla will be fine. I meant would you like to come to the potluck supper and presentation with Darla and me." He leaned back against the granite counter and waited, lips tilted up in a quirky smile.

Susannah debated. It might be okay for tonight, but later, when the baby was showing more, everyone would wonder. Maybe the speculation would ruin his business and then she'd be responsible...but she was tired of hiding out at Connie's or the mall.

"I didn't realize it was such a major decision," he chuckled.

"I would like to go," she said so fast her tongue couldn't rescind it. "Thank you very much."

"You're welcome." Just for a second, he gazed at her in a way that made her face feel warm. Then his attention moved to his sister as she came back into the room. "Ready?" he asked.

"Yes. I put the soda in the trunk," Darla told him. She

giggled as she told Susannah, "Davy bought root beer for his boys to have when they visit, but they don't like it. Neither do I," she said, her nose wrinkling. "We're taking it to the potluck."

"And if they don't like it, they can pass it on," David said, urging them toward the car. "I'm sick of looking at those cases taking up room in the garage." He stowed the cooler, then held the car doors while Darla and Susannah climbed inside. Once seated, he grinned at her. "Just one of the bad choices *I've* made," he said as they pulled out of the driveway and headed toward the church.

"What about that man you hired to put the carpet in your office?" Darla asked.

David winced. "Okay, two bad choices," he admitted. "He was the worst carpet layer I've ever seen. Can we let it go?"

But Darla was beginning to enjoy herself and Susannah was, too.

"Mrs. Peter's Christmas sweater?" Darla giggled.

"I didn't know she was allergic to cashmere!" he protested.

"Asking Mr. Hornby to fix the mess you made in the garden?" Darla laughed out loud at the chagrin on his face.

"He wasn't supposed to do it all at once." David's pained look spoke volumes. "I wasn't trying to kill him." Darla laughed until they pulled into the church parking lot.

"What about the cat?" she asked, ignoring his groan.

When David refused to answer, Susannah asked Darla, "What about a cat?"

"He got me a gift. A sweet cat, all white. I called her Snow White 'cause she loved to sleep." Darla's face softened, her dark eyes began to glow. "Davy *said* she was a special cat, that she'd be my best friend. That was when I was really sick. I had to stay home and I hurt a lot. Holding Snow White made me feel better."

They'd arrived at the church. David climbed out of the car, but after one look at Darla's face, he shook his head and left them to carry the cooler into the church. Susannah nudged the girl's arm.

"What happened?" This she had to hear.

"Well, Snow White ran away a whole bunch of times. If Mrs. Peter's opened the door, that cat would race outside and she didn't come back." Darla frowned. "I didn't hurt her or anything."

"I know you wouldn't do that," Susannah assured her.

"No, I wouldn't," Darla huffed. "Well, every time Snow White would run away, Davy would go and look for her. Sometimes it took a long time and I could hear him calling and calling. But he always brought her home. Except one night."

Surely the poor thing hadn't been hurt? Susannah bit her lip. She had a special affection for cats, honed by years of sitting in the barn on her foster family's farm, crying over her mother's refusal to answer her letters.

"It's okay, Susannah, you don't have to be sad." Darla bent her head trying to see into Susannah's eyes. "It's not bad," she rushed to reassure.

"You'd better explain, Dar. I can see she already thinks the worst." David leaned against the car while Darla explained.

"Well, Snow White had babies. She didn't want to stay with me. She just wanted to come to my house and eat so she could feed her babies," Darla explained. "Mrs. Murphy was away and the boy she hired didn't take care of Snow White very well so Snow White had to take care of her family herself."

"By mooching off of us," David grumbled.

"When Mrs. Murphy came home and saw Davy picking up Snow White and carrying her away, she got really mad at him. It was her cat, you see. She called the police and she followed him home. She was yelling and her face was all red."

"How was I supposed to know it was her cat? I didn't even know the woman, let alone that she had a cat." Obviously disgruntled, David picked a fuzz ball off his sweater. "It was wandering around, yowling all the time. I thought we could give it a home. I paid over a hundred dollars for shots for that animal."

"That's okay, Davy. Snow White was grateful." Darla patted his arm.

"Well, Mrs. Murphy wasn't." His averted his face. "Calling the police on me was a bit extreme."

"Yes, that must have been—er—challenging." Susannah struggled to suppress her mirth.

"Snow White scratched Davy and tore his pants. Then Mrs. Murphy hit him with a broom." Darla reached out and touched him. "I'm sorry, Davy."

"So am I," David said in an aggrieved tone. "I fed that great hulking thing fresh fish for two weeks and neither that cat nor her mistress said thank you even once."

"Snow White still comes over for a visit sometimes," Darla interjected. "But not if Davy's home."

"And don't think I'm unhappy about that." He gave a snort of derision.

Susannah couldn't help it, she burst out laughing. The thought of this big, accomplished, well-respected man avoiding a little white cat made her giggle. She could not imagine him prowling the streets, calling the cat and enduring all manner of indignities from Mrs. Murphy.

"Now that you know my mistakes, let's go inside. I'd like to eat some of that food before it's gone," David said with a hint of a grin in his eyes.

He walked around the car to open Susannah's door and help her out. She was very conscious of David's helping hand under her elbow.

She walked up the sidewalk with David and Darla, mentally steeling herself for what was to come. This was one reason why she'd refused to go to church with Connie; she feared people would start asking questions that she didn't want to answer.

But no one asked her a thing. David introduced her by name as their friend, and that seemed to be enough for people. Everyone she spoke to welcomed her and invited her to enjoy herself. And she did.

It was only later, when Susannah was seated in a pew beside David that she began to feel self-conscious as the speaker, Rick Green, talked about God's love.

"It was my privilege to teach these people that nothing they've done could erase the love of God," he said confidently. "Nothing."

He spoke at length about conditions along the river and the many trials he endured in his work. His pictures were a graphic testimony to his endurance. But Susannah kept hearing her mother's voice screaming condemnation.

It's your fault. It's your fault.

As always, a punch of pain accompanied the words and she squeezed her eyes closed to brace against it.

The social worker had insisted the deaths of her sisters, Cara and Misty, weren't her fault. But even after all these years, in the recesses of her heart, Susannah couldn't rid herself of the guilt that dogged her.

It *was* her fault. She *should* have been there.

She was a failure.

A hand pressed against hers, warm, comforting.

She opened her eyes and found David staring at her, concern in his gaze.

"Are you all right?" he whispered.

She dredged up a smile and nodded as she eased her fingers from his, forcing herself to pretend a calm she didn't feel. Why did his touch affect her so deeply?

After several moments of scrutiny he finally returned his attention to the speaker, but he kept giving her little sideways looks, as if he thought she might faint or do something equally inappropriate.

"Hear me tonight," Rick Green said softly. "There is nothing God wouldn't do for you. In fact, He's already done it by sending His son to die for you. All you have to do is accept His love."

By the time the meeting broke up, Susannah had regained her equilibrium. She was able to tease Darla and smile at David who still looked concerned. Connie and Wade joined them.

"You must have loved your trip down to the Amazon, judging by those amazing pictures," Susannah said to Wade.

"We did," Wade agreed. "Especially the piranhas." He held up a threatening hand and began tickling the back of Darla's neck. In a fit of giggles, she wiggled away.

"You know, we never did get to finish that trip because of Dad's heart attack," David mused. "We should go back sometime."

"I second that." A tall, lean man with sandy blond hair exchanged a complicated handshake with the other two men, hugged Connie and Darla and then held out a hand to Susannah. "I'm Jared Hornby," he said.

"Oh. I've heard a lot about you." Susannah shook his hand. She could see the easy camaraderie between the three men. "Darla shared some information, too," she added.

"Aw, kiddo! Can't you ever keep a secret," Jared asked Darla and grinned when she said, "No."

"I'm not putting money in that basket. I just don't agree with raising money to feed kids who live in this country." A shrill voice broke through their conversation, carrying from the foyer into the sanctuary. "Did you see the pictures of those children in the Amazon, how poor they are? It seems criminal to me that in this country of plenty, we give our hard-earned money to people who have social assistance and all kinds of government handouts. If they won't look after their own children, then the government can take over. Not a dime should go to that Mary's Kids Foundation."

"Uh-oh," Connie murmured. Mary's Kids was one of the charities she'd recently set up with a friend to help kids on the streets of Tucson. "I'll go—"

"I'm afraid I have to disagree with you there, Mrs. Beesom." David's voice carried clearly, his tone calm. "Needy kids are needy wherever they are, whether in Tucson or the Amazon. We should be ashamed that we've let American children get to the point where they are so desperate to eat that they have to rob and steal. It's disgraceful that in America a child isn't cared for by the whole community."

Susannah moved with the rest toward the foyer. She couldn't help admiring David's casual stance. There was no hint of anger in his voice or manner, though she saw a flicker of golden fire in the depths of his eyes.

"Disgraceful? Well, that's just silly. They have mothers and fathers," Mrs. Beesom blustered.

"That isn't the point," he said quietly. "The point is that there are children hurting around the world. It's our God-given responsibility to do whatever we can to alleviate the hurt of children whenever we can, no matter where they live."

"But—"

David wasn't finished.

"Thank God Connie Abbot has taken it upon herself to show God's love to the children of Tucson, just as this gentleman has been showing love to those he meets in the Amazon. We should all be doing more to support both of them."

After a couple of coughs and a few murmured amens, the foyer quickly cleared, but not before people dropped donations into both baskets.

Susannah followed Connie and Wade outside. The group paused in the parking lot.

"Look guys, I'm so sorry," Connie murmured, her embarrassment obvious. "I had no idea that would happen. I should have removed everything about Mary's Kids from the bulletin board."

"Don't be silly, Connie," David said. "She should have thought first."

"I'm sure David saw it as an opportunity to try and educate narrow-minded people rather than let their bigotry go unchallenged, didn't you, old man?" Jared slapped him on the back. "You always were a defender of the weak."

"I'm not a saint." David brushed away the praise. "What say we go out for coffee? I'm buying."

"But I don't drink coffee, Davy," Darla complained.

Everyone burst out laughing. David assured his sister

they'd find her something to drink. As they drove to the coffee house, Susannah couldn't help but replay the scene in her mind.

She'd always seen David as cool and distant. But his defense of Connie's charity tonight showed her a new side. She assumed he thought her stupid, beneath him. But the truth was, he had never verbally condemned or judged her. Maybe she was misreading him, and shutting him out without giving him a chance to show who he really was.

David was great with Darla—understanding and gentle. He went out of his way to empathize with his sister's issues. He was exactly the kind of man who could listen and then help you figure out the next step. Connie was a great friend, but Susannah was sure that if she told her the plans she had to adopt her baby, Connie would try to change her mind. Susannah needed another confidant, someone who could advise her about adoption. Someone who wouldn't try to sway her, who would listen and even help

Tonight, David had shown he could empathize.

Tomorrow, Susannah would find out if he would help her.

Chapter Seven

"Surprise!"

On Saturday evening, David stared at the array of food on his kitchen counter and was dumbfounded.

He'd never expected this when he'd called to ask Susannah if she and Darla wanted to join him and the boys for dinner.

"I thought a barbeque might be more fun for your little brothers than being stuck in a stuffy restaurant." Susannah's cheeks burned a hot pink. But whether from effort or something else, he couldn't tell.

"We made a dinner," Darla told him, beaming with pride.

"You certainly did." He glanced at his three little brothers who were eyeing the fixings for a wonderful grilled meal with huge eyes. "But I'm sure they'd rather go out, wouldn't you, guys?" he teased.

"No way." Their team had won the hockey game and they were high on excitement. "Can we have both a burger and a hot dog?" the eldest asked in awe. "And some of the other stuff?"

"If you can find room after all that junk food you ate." He told them to wash up, then went out to the patio.

David couldn't remember the last time he'd worked so hard over a grill—nor the last time he'd heard so much laughter in his backyard.

Nor had he ever seen Susannah so happy. She insisted on dashing around, making sure everyone had enough to eat until David finally ordered her to sit down and enjoy her own meal.

She had a way with the boys. She didn't duck their questions about her baby, or try to change the subject. She answered honestly and they seemed to appreciate that. In fact, David was gratified to see them ask her to remain at the table while they cleared the dishes. He stacked the dishwasher himself, so he could listen in on their conversation.

"Boy, David, Susannah's sure pretty. What happened to her husband?" Caden, the eldest, asked.

"He died, I think." David wasn't sure he wanted to reveal more about Susannah without her permission. "Thanks for pitching in, guys."

"It was nothing." Charles, the youngest, peered out the window where Darla and Susannah sat together on the deck swing. "Does she live here?"

"No. She comes over to watch Darla when I can't be here," he explained.

"Darla's different than the last time we saw her," Cory said. "She doesn't look so sad. And she didn't yell even once."

"Yeah. She's fun," Caden agreed. "And she's pretty now."

Like she wasn't before? David choked back his brotherly ire and picked up the platter of cookies Susannah had left on the top of the fridge.

"We've barely got enough time to eat these before I have

to get you home," he said as he shepherded them outside. "Your mom said no later than eight, remember?"

They grumbled but devoured the cookies as they asked Darla about the butterfly exhibit. To David's surprise, his sister knew a lot about it and was able to clearly explain what she and Susannah had seen.

"I won't be more than half an hour," he told Susannah before leaving. "The boys' place isn't too far away."

"We'll be here," Susannah promised. She hugged each of the boys, then handed Caden a bag. "Extra cookies in case you want a snack tomorrow. And there might be some fudge brownies in there, too," she added with a wink.

"Really?" Caden's eyes widened. "Thanks a lot."

David shooed them out to the car, but stopped when Susannah's hand pressed his arm.

"They're not allergic or anything, are they?" she asked.

"To chocolate?" He grinned. "More like addicted. Thanks for doing that. It was very thoughtful. They don't get treats like that very often."

"It was mostly Darla," she said. "I just helped."

He thought about that as he took the boys home. It seemed Susannah "just helped" everyone. He knew from Wade that Susannah took over meals when their housekeeper had the day off. Which was a good thing because Connie, for all her achievements, was no cook.

Susannah "just helped" Darla take swimming lessons, with the result that Darla had zipped through the first four levels and was almost done with the fifth. She'd "just helped" his little brothers enjoy a wonderful barbecue in a homey atmosphere, gently urging them out of their shells, until all three boys had lost their shyness.

Susannah Wells was quite a woman.

David pulled into the garage and waited for the door to close.

He liked her. He really liked her. Susannah didn't pretend to be someone else. She didn't seem to bear a grudge, though she had plenty of reason to. She was honest with Darla, yet wonderfully calm and soothing.

Like a sister.

Only David didn't think of Susannah as a sister.

Careful.

He found her inside, staring into space.

"Oh, you're back," she said, startled, as if she'd been deep in thought. "Darla's upstairs having a bath."

"Good. She was pretty sticky from all the cookies." Something was going on. He could see it in her eyes.

"Do you—"

"Could I talk to you?" she blurted. "Confidentially, as a lawyer?"

"Okay," he said cautiously.

"I'll pay you and everything," she promised, "but I don't want what I say to leave this room." A desperate look washed over her delicate features, as if she'd been brooding over something and finally felt driven to bring it to light.

"As your lawyer, I'm forbidden to release anything you tell me to anyone else," he assured her. "Would you like some tea while we talk?" He had to do something to try to ease her discomfort. The uncertainty in her voice touched him. He wanted to help her, to ease the strain in her lovely eyes. He wanted to give her some of the joy she so freely encouraged in others.

"Yes. Please." Susannah waited until he'd made the tea and set everything on the table in front of them.

"Talk to me, Susannah. Please? I promise I'll try to help," he said when silence continued to reign.

"I need to know how to give up my baby for adoption."

The question hit him squarely in the gut.

Give away her child?

David forced his face to remain neutral, but inside his brain churned with questions.

"I can't keep it, that's for sure." She twisted her fingers together, staring at them as if she hoped to find answers there.

"Do you have someone in mind? Connie and Wade?" he guessed.

"No!" Susannah stared at him. "You can't tell them about this. Not a word."

"I'm not going to say anything to anyone, Susannah. I promise. Relax." He laid his hands over hers to help her calm down. "It's just—this is a bit of a surprise. I don't understand. Maybe you could explain some more?"

"No." She yanked her hands away and jumped to her feet. "I shouldn't have bothered you. I'll figure things out. But please, don't tell Connie."

"Susannah." David saw a myriad of conflicting emotions on her face. He could tell she was really struggling with her decision, with her feelings. "As your lawyer, I *can't* talk to Connie or anyone else. That's the law." He rose, touched her shoulder. "I really want to help you. But in order to give you the best advice I can, I need to know more about what's driving your decision."

She frowned, her uncertainty obvious. His heart gave a lurch as he watched her struggle to find some trust.

"Let's just talk. No decisions, no judging—just talking," he coaxed quietly. "You don't have to decide anything right now. But I'd like to know what you're thinking and feeling. This is a big decision."

He found himself holding his breath. Would she trust him?

"I know exactly how big it is," she said. Finally she sat down. "I've been fighting it for a while. But I think the best thing for my baby would be for me to find a good family to raise it."

So now he was going to arrange an adoption?

So much for not getting involved, buddy.

With grim determination, David shut down the voice in his head. The truth was he was already involved in Susannah's life way more than he'd ever imagined he'd be. Over the past few weeks he'd caught himself watching to be sure she drank the freshly squeezed juice with which he'd insisted Mrs. Peters stock the fridge, and that she'd sampled the variety of organic fruit he kept buying at the health food store. He'd even checked the house for repairs that needed doing so she wouldn't trip on something, or hurt herself.

If he had to, David could recite every detail Darla had ever mentioned about Susannah's baby. Yeah, he wasn't getting involved.

"I would prefer if the adopters didn't know about my mistakes." The words emerged in a quiet, painful whisper.

"Okay." He nodded. "Now tell me why."

"Why?" She gave a half laugh, chewed on her bottom lip then looked directly at him. "Because my past is not the kind of fairy-tale reading a child needs."

"I meant why do you want to have someone adopt your baby?" he clarified.

"Isn't it obvious?" She frowned at him. "I can't be the kind of mother this baby needs."

"Why not?" he asked, pouring tea for both of them.

"I shouldn't even be a mother," she whispered.

"And yet you will be."

"I know." She nodded soberly. "But I can't provide the best environment for a child." Her eyes brimmed with shame.

"You're not a criminal. You haven't hurt anyone. You like kids and you're good with people." He shook his head. "I don't understand what possibly disqualifies you as a mother."

"Look around, David," she said, a tinge of bitterness edging her voice. "Look at what your parents provided for you and Darla. I'll bet your mother stayed home to care for you, didn't she?"

"Actually she was a partner in my father's firm." David smiled at the cascade of memories. "Best litigator I've ever known. But she would not do wills or family law. Absolutely refused."

"Oh." Susannah swallowed. "Well, anyway, I meant your parents provided a home and income for their children. They had a reputation that covered you."

"You have a bad reputation?" he asked, half in jest.

Susannah's eyes, dark and swirling with secrets, met his. After a moment she nodded. "Did Connie ever tell you about our foster home?" She glanced away, focusing on something outside the window.

"A little. How much she was loved, cared for. How much she appreciated what they did for her. That kind of thing. Why?" He didn't understand where this was going.

"I was sent to that foster home after a house fire— which was my fault." Susannah straightened. Her shoulders went back. Her jaw tightened. "Do you know where I was when the fire started?"

David gave a grim shake of his head.

"I snuck into a theater," she said, her voice brimming

with unshed tears. "I ran away. My—mother was at home. She got badly burned in that fire, because of me."

Years of past misery now darkened her gorgeous eyes to green-black shadows. Pain oozed from her. David wanted to help but he didn't know the words to dissolve this kind of agony. It had festered too long.

"Susannah—"

"There's another reason I can't keep my baby." Susannah dragged her hand away from his and tucked it under her.

"What is that?" David asked, longing to hold her, to ease her obvious distress.

"My mother was not a good mother. I might be like her."

David wanted to laugh at the utter ridiculousness of it. But Susannah's face made it clear how serious she was.

"You are not like her, Susannah," he said, certain of that truth.

"I don't drink, but maybe—"

He shook his head and continued shaking it as she listed other faults she thought she might have inherited.

"No way."

"How can you say that?" A hint of defiance colored her voice. "You barely know me."

"I actually know you quite well, Susannah Wells." He smiled at her blink of surprise. "You are sweet and gentle with Darla when she's acting her worst. You go out of your way to make three boys you don't even know the most fantastic barbecue. You listen when I whine and complain and you never stop looking for opportunities to help anyone who needs a hand." He touched her cheek. "You'll make a wonderful mother."

She was silent a long time, head bent as she thought about it. But when she lifted her golden head and looked at him, David knew she hadn't heard him, not in her heart where the insecurities had taken root.

"You don't know what kind of mother I'll be, and neither do I. And I'm not going to risk the life of my baby. My track record isn't good. I'm not worthy of motherhood and I won't risk my baby." She gathered her jacket. "So are you going to help me figure out how to do an adoption, or should I find someone else?"

David rose, determined to make her see herself the way others saw her.

"In the past you made some bad choices, Susannah," he said seriously. "Maybe partly because of what you were told and partly because you were afraid to expect better of yourself."

"So?" Her long hair twisted up on the top of her head lent her a quiet dignity, its sheen a golden crown under the kitchen lights.

"I wish you could believe that your past doesn't determine your future. I wish you could let go of all those feelings of unworthiness," he told her, letting his soul speak. "You have so much inside you to give. You just need to trust God to help you and give yourself another chance."

"God isn't going to be bothered with me."

"God is bothered with everyone," he assured her quietly.

"And what if I blow that chance? I've done it a hundred times before. What happens to my baby then?" she challenged him. Then she cleared her voice. "Are you going to help me with this adoption or not?"

"Of course I'll help you. After all you've done for us, I would feel ashamed not to. You're the best thing I could ever have wished for Darla." He bent and brushed his lips against her silky cheek, surprised by the rush of longing he felt to make her world better. "Thank you."

She lifted a hand and touched her cheek where he'd kissed her.

"You're welcome," she whispered.

Then she was gone.

David stood in the kitchen and let his spirit talk to God because he couldn't find the words to convey all that was in his heart.

Sometime later he became aware he was not alone.

"Davy?"

"Yes, sweetie?"

Darla stood behind him, her face very sad.

"What's wrong?"

"Why does Susannah want to give away her baby, Davy?"

"That's a secret, sis. You can't ever talk about it. Not to anyone."

"Okay. But I love Susannah's baby."

"I know." He gathered her in his arms and let her cry on his shoulder, his sweet baby sister who was alive and getting better every day thanks to a small woman who oozed love.

Oh, Susannah, his heart wept.

"I'll only talk about it to God," Darla promised, sniffing. "He'll help. Let's ask Him."

So right then and there they prayed for Susannah and the child she was afraid to love.

But even that didn't ease David's concern over the heart-wrenching choices Susannah was determined to make.

"There's got to be something I can do," he prayed after

Darla had gone to bed. "Show me some way to help her avoid making this tragic mistake."

Being Susannah's friend/lawyer hardly seemed enough.

Chapter Eight

"I can't believe you actually brought my sister to this place."

All signs of last week's gentle, understanding man whom Susannah had trusted with her deepest secrets was gone. She'd felt so close to him, even more so after that kiss. Her brain said it was all part of his thank-you, but her heart had sensed the tenderness in him, felt the gentleness of his eyes when his lips touched her. What a difference a week made.

Susannah tried to explain.

"They have a wonderful program with pottery here. Darla can finally dig her fingers into the clay and create as she wants to. She's ecstatic."

"Do you see who these people are? Drunks. Addicts. Criminals. Pottery is fine, but here?" He cast a disparaging glance at the disheveled young man working beside Darla's table. "He looks like he's been living on the street."

"He has. Burt's had some bad luck." Susannah hated the way David looked at the man—because Burt could have been her not so long ago.

"I'm sure he has." David took her arm and steered

her to a corner. "This could be dangerous, Susannah. I don't like Darla in a place like this. You know she's had a couple of tantrums this past week."

"She's not going to be perfect all the time," she replied. "No one is."

"I didn't say *perfect*." He tightened his lips as a woman walked past, talking to herself in a high, screechy voice. "What if Darla gets upset and acts up? One of them could take exception and attack her. There is mental illness here."

"You're being ridiculous," she snapped, irritated by his attitude. "Connie's come here to New Horizons many times. No one's ever bothered her."

"Connie isn't a nineteen-year-old girl who—"

"Hi, Davy." Darla wound her arm through his, her face beaming with happiness. "This is my friend, Oliver. He likes to make pottery, too, but Oliver is way better at it than I am."

"Hey." Oliver gave David the once-over, then shook his head. "He's mad," he said to Darla. "I told you he was."

"Davy?" Darla shifted so she could stare into his eyes. "Are you mad?"

"He is," Oliver asserted. "His face is tight and his eyes are all crinkled and mad-looking. I'm leaving." He trotted to the far side of the room where he sat down in a chair and watched them.

"Why are you mad, Davy? Oliver is my friend. I thought you'd be nice to him." Storm clouds rolled across Darla's face.

"We *were* nice, Darla," Susannah intervened before David could give voice to his thoughts about this place. "I'm sure Oliver is fine. Can we show David what you made this afternoon? I think it's going to be beautiful."

After a sidelong look at her friend, Darla proudly led the way to the massive vase she'd begun creating from coils of clay.

"Oliver showed me how to put them together. Oliver knows a lot about clay." Darla glanced around the room, but Oliver had disappeared.

"He was a sculptor," Susannah murmured for David's ears only. "His fiancée died in a car crash. He's had a hard time since then."

"It's very nice, Dar." David walked around the piece. "How big is it going to be?"

"Big. That's why Oliver has to help," Darla said, her forehead pleated in a frown.

"Why? You're the one creating it." David didn't have to say he disapproved of Oliver. It was there in his tone.

And Darla picked up on it.

"You don't know about Oliver, Davy. You think 'cause he's different than other people that he isn't smart. But he's really smart about pottery." Darla pointed. "That's his work."

Susannah felt a ping of satisfaction at the surprise filling David's eyes as he studied the massive sculpture.

"Very nice."

"I told you, Oliver is good." Darla touched her work with pride. "I'm going to be good, too."

"You already are," Susannah said.

"You have to put pots in the kiln. But this pot will be too high," Darla explained. "Oliver is going to show me how to make it so I can fire it and put it together after. No one will even know it was two pieces."

"I see. Well, I guess you would have to know kilns to

know how to do that," he admitted. "Are you finished for today?"

"Not quite," Susannah intervened. "We need to pay the course fee today. This week was just a trial period. That's why I asked you to meet us here. I thought you'd like to see what Darla would be doing."

"Fine," he said in an inflexible voice. "But I don't think we'll pay the fee today. We should talk about it first."

"But, Davy, I can't come and work here if we don't pay." Darla's voice rose with each word.

Susannah knew David expected her to do something to help Darla regain control, but the truth was, she was angry, too. She'd spent weeks searching for some way Susannah could make pottery with the guidance of someone who knew about clay and could help her realize her dreams.

Now that they'd found it, David objected because it wasn't up to his social standards?

"Come on," he said, reaching for her arm. "Let's go home and discuss it."

"No." Darla glared at him and yanked her arm away. "I want you to give the money for classes so I can come back here." Her voice had risen but she was not yet in the full throes of a tantrum.

"Excuse me?"

They turned as one to stare at the small, wizened gentleman who stood behind David.

"Are you having a problem here, Susannah?" He grinned at her, his almost toothless smile lighting up his wrinkled and worn face. "Can't have that baby of yours upset, now can we?"

"I think we're okay, Robert." She smiled, loving the

way he'd rushed to her defense. Nobody but Connie had done that before.

"Well, you tell me if there's a problem, because we don't want arguing and fighting here." He waved a hand encompassing the room. "People come here to feel safe. If this man is bothering you—"

"This is Darla's brother, David Foster. David, this is Robert. He's a friend of mine."

"Robert. What line of work are you in?" David's tone offended Susannah, but she kept silent.

"Oh, I retired years ago. I just come here for a cup of coffee and a chat. Susannah will tell you I like to chat. And do woodworking." He winked at Susannah. "One of these days I'm going to get this little mama working on the lathe."

"It's nice of you to offer, Robert," Susannah said, patting his hand. "But I think I should learn something about pottery first. Darla's so good at it."

"Excuse us. We have to go." David waited until the old man wished them a good day, then turned to Darla. "You can make a scene if you want to, but I am leaving. This is not a place where you should be. I want you to go home. Now." He glared at Susannah, then turned and walked out of the room.

"Davy!" Darla wailed.

"We'll talk to him at home," Susannah whispered to Darla, concerned by the girl's white face. "You can tell him all about the center and explain it."

"Davy doesn't want me to explain," Darla said, tears edging her voice. She walked out of the room biting her lip to keep control. "Davy's already decided that I can't come here. He's embarrassed of me."

It was pointless to argue with her—especially since Susannah wasn't sure she was wrong. So she said nothing. She drove the girl home and helped her carry in her clay tools before hugging her goodbye.

"I have to go now, but it will be all right, Darla," she whispered, hoping she was right.

"I'm going to pray and ask God to help," Darla said before she fled upstairs.

Susannah bit her lip and turned to leave.

"Don't leave yet. I want to talk to you." David motioned to his study.

"Fine." Susannah followed him, tired and wishing she could crawl into a hot bath instead.

She smoothed a hand over her hair as she sank into the nearest chair. She noticed the clay stuck to her shoe, the streak of brown on her sleeve.

David sat down behind his desk, elegant, completely unmussed. That irritated her even more.

"Well? What do you need to say?" She crossed her feet. "It's been a long day. I'm tired. I'd like to go home."

"I want to know what on earth possessed you to take my sister to that place," he demanded, his voice icy.

"Pottery. Pottery possessed me," she shot back. "That and your sister's love of it. Which is something you seem to have difficulty grasping. If you'd only seen her face while she was working," she mourned.

"She can do pottery somewhere else." There was no give in his tone.

"That's the thing, David." Susannah was tired of his attitude. "She can't. Other programs have already begun. They won't allow her to join late."

"So she waits."

"And does what? Goes to more girls' clubs where she is miserable?" Susannah rose. "I suggest you think long and hard about denying her this opportunity."

"Did you even look at Oliver? Didn't you recognize him?" David's scathing tone left her in no doubt that he had recognized the sculptor.

"I told you he was well-known for his work with clay." Susannah fiddled with the strap on her purse, wishing she'd hadn't already eaten the apple she'd put in her bag earlier.

"Oh, Oliver is famous for more than pottery." A smug look washed over David's face. "He has some actions pending for damaging a building downtown. That's what I mean about being unsuitable."

"You don't even know the circumstances and yet you've already passed sentence on him." Susannah shook her head. "I wonder how judgmental you'd be if it was Darla who'd damaged something and was being charged. I wonder if you wouldn't make sure she got all the chances you could give her or if you'd just toss her away the way you seem to be willing to cross Oliver off your 'worthwhile human being' list." Another thought intruded, making her even angrier. "Or is it me you're really afraid of, of my being among like kind like that? Maybe I'll revert to my old habits."

"In my opinion," he said, his voice harsh and unyielding, "it is a bad decision on your part to make friends there and associate with those kinds of people."

"Those kind of people." She smiled. "I *am* those kind of people, David. Worthless, useless—society's write-offs."

"I didn't mean—"

"Yes, you did, David." Susannah had to get out of there before she said something horrible, something that she couldn't retract. Most of all, she had to forget the man who had so tenderly kissed her cheek.

She held his gaze for a moment more, then left, closing

the door silently behind her. She walked home slowly, allowing the tears to fall without even trying to stop them.

So now she knew what he really thought. She'd suspected it all along—so why did it hurt so much that this man she admired more than any she'd ever known could write her off as worthless so easily?

David couldn't sleep.

Over and over he kept hearing her.

I am that kind of people. Worthless. Useless. Society's write-offs.

He'd argued when Susannah claimed herself unworthy to be a mother—but he'd just confirmed her judgment.

Irritated with himself and the persistent squawk of his brain telling him not to get involved, David went downstairs, brewed some tea and carried it to the family room. To his surprise, Darla was there.

"What are you doing up?" he asked.

She didn't answer. Her deep brown eyes studied him for a long time, long enough to make him shift uncomfortable.

"I don't like you today," she said finally. "You were mean to Susannah. She tried really hard to help me, and you were rude."

"I wasn't trying to be rude," he began, but Darla wouldn't let him get away with that.

"Yes, you were. You wanted to make yourself better than all the other people at the center. That was rude."

When had his sister acquired such understanding?

"I was afraid for you," he admitted simply.

"Don't you know Susannah? Don't you know she would never let anything happen to me? Even if it was going to, which it wasn't. The center is a good place."

W

e'd like to send you two free books to introduce you to the *Love Inspired*® series. Your two books have a combined cover price of $11.00 or more in the U.S. and $13.00 or more in Canada, but they are yours free! We'll even send you two wonderful surprise gifts. You can't lose!

Each of your **FREE** books is filled with joy, faith and traditional values as men and women open their hearts to each other and join together on a spiritual journey.

GET 2 FREE BOOKS!

Love Inspired

YES! Please send me the 2 FREE Love Inspired® books and 2 free gifts for which I qualify. I understand that I am under no obligation to purchase anything further, as explained on the back of this card.

affix free books sticker here

About how many NEW paperback fiction books have you purchased in the past 3 months?

❏ 0-2
FC66

❏ 3-6
FC7J

❏ 7 or more
FC7U

❏ I prefer the regular-print edition
105/305 IDL

❏ I prefer the larger-print edition
122/322 IDL

Please Print

FIRST NAME

LAST NAME

ADDRESS

APT.#

CITY

STATE/PROV.

ZIP/POSTAL CODE

▼ DETACH AND MAIL CARD TODAY! ▼

® and ™ are trademarks owned and used by the trademark owner and/or its licensee.
© 2010 LOVE INSPIRED BOOKS
Printed in the U.S.A.

(LI-LA-11)

The Reader Service — Here's How it Works:

Accepting your 2 free books and 2 free mystery gifts places you under no obligation to buy anything. You may keep the books and gifts and return the shipping statement marked "cancel." If you do not cancel, about a month later we will send you 6 additional books and bill you just $4.24 each for the regular-print edition or $4.74 each for the larger-print edition in the U.S. or $4.74 each for the regular-print edition or $5.24 each for the larger-print edition in Canada. That's a savings of at least 23% off the cover price. It's quite a bargain! Shipping and handling is just 50¢ per book in the U.S. and 75¢ per book in Canada.* You may cancel at any time, but if you choose to continue, every month we'll send you 6 more books, which you may either purchase at the discount price or return to us and cancel your subscription. *Terms and prices subject to change without notice. Prices do not include applicable taxes. Sales tax applicable in N.Y. Canadian residents will be charged applicable taxes. Offer not valid in Quebec. All orders subject to credit approval. Books received may not be as shown. Credit or debit balances in a customer's account(s) may be offset by any other outstanding balance owed by or to the customer. Please allow 4 to 6 weeks for delivery. Offer available while quantities last.

▲ If offer card is missing write to: The Reader Service, P.O. Box 1867, Buffalo, NY 14240-1867 or visit www.ReaderService.com ▲

BUSINESS REPLY MAIL
FIRST-CLASS MAIL   PERMIT NO. 717   BUFFALO, NY

POSTAGE WILL BE PAID BY ADDRESSEE

THE READER SERVICE
PO BOX 1867
BUFFALO NY 14240-9952

NO POSTAGE
NECESSARY
IF MAILED
IN THE
UNITED STATES

Her voice touched a chord deep inside David and reverberated through his mind. For the first time since the accident, Darla was confronting him with her anger instead of throwing a tantrum.

"Susannah is the best friend I ever had and you're going to make her go away."

"I hope not." That was the last thing he wanted.

"You made her feel like I feel when people call me a dummy," Darla said bluntly.

"I never said—"

"And you made our friends at the center feel like that, too. They're not dummies, Davy," she said, her face earnest. "And it doesn't matter if you say it or not. When you talk the way you did, they know what you mean."

How could he argue with that? He'd been a jerk.

"Susannah knows that. She talks to Oliver and Burt and the others like she talks to me, like she talks to you." Darla bowed her head. "When she talks to us, she makes us feel strong. She makes us feel like we can do things. Lots of things."

Meaning he didn't do that for her?

"You're my brother and I love you lots, but sometimes you say things that hurt people," Darla said, her voice grave. "Today you made Susannah feel bad and I don't like that. You should apologize."

"But—"

"My Sunday school teacher said God wants people to help one another."

"Darla, it's not that simple."

"Everybody at the center likes Susannah because she knows that sometimes you just need help." She narrowed her gaze. "I don't think they like you, Davy."

"Sweetie," he said, "it's not that I didn't like them."

"Then why do you think they'll do bad things? When I make mistakes, do you think I'll do bad things?"

"No, but—"

"Susannah says everybody makes mistakes." *Even you,* Darla's eyes seemed to say. "But people can change. That's what Susannah says."

Susannah. She had pitted his own sister against him now.

Susannah didn't do that. I did.

"The Bible says you're supposed to love everybody, no matter what. Doesn't it, Davy?" she challenged.

"Yes, but—"

"Then you should have love in your heart for Oliver and Burt and Susannah and everyone. You should expect them to do good things, not bad things." She crossed her arms over her chest, her face set.

Darla had just summed up the Christian life in action.

Shamed by his words and his attitude, and the fact that God had used his little sister to show him his own arrogance, David rose and moved to sit beside Darla.

"You know what?" he said as he took her hand.

"What?" she demanded.

"I think you're the smartest woman I know."

"Really?" A beatific smile lit up her face.

He kissed her cheek and hugged her as he praised God for Darla. "I'll apologize to Susannah tomorrow."

"Good. And Davy?" She pulled back, her face worried.

"Yes, sweetie?" He tucked a strand of her glossy hair behind one ear. "What is it?"

"It's her birthday tomorrow. Connie told me she's having a surprise party for Susannah tomorrow night and we're invited." Darla beamed with the excitement of keeping a secret. "I wasn't going to tell you if you were mean, but if you apologize, that's okay. Can we get Susannah a gift?"

"We'll go in the morning," he promised. "Now, let's get some sleep."

"I already know what I want to give Susannah," Darla said. "A dress for Thanksgiving. That green one we saw."

"That will be nice."

"Uh-huh." She flung her arms around him and hugged him so tightly David almost lost his balance. "Good night, Davy," she called.

He spent a long time thinking about the nurturer that was Susannah Wells, and about how he'd treated her. And about that kiss he had planted on her cheek…

She was amazing. Nothing seemed to faze the woman. She thrived on helping anyone who needed her.

How could such a nurturing woman ever give up her child?

She couldn't. It would haunt her for the rest of her life.

David knew then that he couldn't help her find adoptive parents for her baby. He wanted Susannah to keep the child, to make a new life for both of them, a life of second chances.

He'd talk to her about that tomorrow. Right after he apologized.

Chapter Nine

"Connie, you shouldn't have done this!" Susannah said, looking at the gifts piled in the living room. The dining table was set with fancy dishes.

"It's your birthday and we're having a party. Get over it." Connie grinned.

"But you're having your Thanksgiving party tomorrow night." Susannah wished she hadn't spent the afternoon sleeping—perhaps she could have put a stop to all this fuss. "This is a lot of extra work."

"It's not work. It's fun." Connie grabbed Susannah's hands and whirled her around. She stopped abruptly. "Oops, sorry. I keep forgetting this little one makes you dizzy." Tenderly she set her hand over Susannah's ever-increasing baby bump. "What a miracle."

Her baby was a miracle? But weren't miracles for those God thought special? Susannah found herself blown away by the thought that God had singled her out, specially gifted her with this child.

Could God have trusted *her* with such a gift?

An instant later the wonder dissolved as reality hit. This baby might be a gift, but it was a gift she couldn't keep.

Guilt assailed Susannah.

"Suze? You feeling okay?"

"Yes, thanks."

"Sure?" Connie's fingertips brushed her forehead before smoothing back her hair. "You don't feel warm."

"I'm absolutely fine." She pulled back. "Don't fuss."

"I have to take care of my best friend, don't I?"

The doorbell rang and a moment later Darla's excited voice, followed by David's lower rumble echoed through the house. Her stomach clenched just as the baby kicked her in the ribs.

"Surprise!" Obviously delighted with her secret, Connie beamed. "I take it Darla didn't squeal on me when she called this morning?"

"Not a word." Susannah hadn't told Connie about her argument with David because she didn't want her friend fighting her battles. She schooled her expression into a placid mask and followed Connie from the room to welcome her guests.

David's gaze caught hers. He smiled at her, eyes melting to butterscotch. There was nothing in his manner to suggest the least problem between them. In fact, he looked happy to see her. Susannah's heart jumped when he continued to stare at her. She swallowed hard and felt a little sick. Not a pregnancy sickness—more a kind of this-can't-be-happening, heart-dropping sickness.

How could he look at her like that, as if he thought she was something special, when she knew he thought she was nothing, nobody? And why did one man get the full package—height, good looks—along with a strong sense of who he was, a sense that would never make him feel unworthy of anything?

"Happy birthday," he said in that low growl she'd become accustomed to. He handed her a small silver box. An envelope was attached. "For you."

His fingers brushed hers. Susannah pulled away, burning at the contact. "Thank you," she whispered.

"I hope you have a great year."

What did that mean? Was that sweet grin a prelude to firing her?

"This is from me." Darla edged in front of him and held out a beautifully wrapped flat box. "Can we open the gifts now?" she asked Connie, impatience showing in her dancing feet.

"Yeah, can we?" Silver echoed, just as excited.

"Why not?" Connie led the way to the family room.

"Open Davy's first," Darla directed.

Embarrassed at being on display, Susannah lifted the lid of the box and found a lovely glass bottle of expensive perfume tucked inside, the kind she sometimes dabbed on at the cosmetics counter but could never afford to buy.

"Thank you," she said, avoiding his gaze.

"You're welcome," David said.

Susannah found nothing in those calm, smooth tones to give away his thoughts. Didn't he feel anything after their argument?

"Now open mine." Darla thrust the box into her hands and flopped down beside her. "I picked it out myself. And I paid for it."

"You shouldn't have spent your money on—oh, my." Susannah lifted out the dress she'd refused to try on in the store the day they'd chosen Darla's new clothes. The green-into-turquoise swirls were just as gorgeous as they had been that day, the fabric just as luxurious. "It's beautiful, Darla. Thank you."

Never had she been more conscious of the shabbiness of her clothes. Connie had tried to help out, but she hadn't had time to sew more than a pair of pants and two simple cotton shirts.

"Put it on," Darla ordered. She pushed the box off Susannah's lap and grabbed her hand. "I want you to put it on."

"But Connie has dinner—" Susannah looked at her friend.

"We can wait," Connie assured her. "It's lovely. Go try it on."

"C'mon, Silver," Darla said, grabbing Connie's stepdaughter's hand.

So up the stairs the three of them went. Susannah was glad to escape. She could feel David's stare boring into her back.

"I might not fit it, Darla," she warned as she peeled off her clothes. "With the baby, I'm—"

"It will fit," Darla assured her. "You'll see."

And in fact, Susannah thought it fit very well, skimming over her body in a swish of fabric. She twirled back and forth in front of the mirror, unable to believe her reflection.

"Put your hair up," Darla ordered.

She clipped her mass of curls to the top of her head with a huge bronze barrette. Then she slipped her feet into a pair of low sandals. They were old, but they suited the dress.

"You look so pretty, Susannah. Let's go show the others," Darla implored. She and Silver raced back downstairs.

Susannah followed more slowly, oddly proud. She knew that for the first time in a very long time, she looked good.

"You're lovely, Susannah." David's low, intimate voice brought a flush to her cheeks.

"It's the dress." Susannah couldn't look at him.

"No." Darla shook her head. "My mom used to say you had to be beautiful inside to be truly beautiful outside." With a quick press, she hugged her then drew away.

Connie coaxed Susannah to sit down and open the rest of her gifts. There was a lovely bracelet from Silver, matching earrings from Connie and Wade, and two new maternity pantsuits, which Connie had sewn.

"It's so much. Thank you, everyone. I think this is the best birthday I've ever had," she said, looking at David as she spritzed a little of the perfume on her wrists.

David's dark-honey gaze locked with hers. Susannah gulped, but she couldn't look away. She felt as if he could see right to the pain she'd tucked deep inside her soul, pain that still stung because her mother couldn't forgive enough to send her only living daughter a birthday greeting. Susannah had tried so hard to gain her forgiveness, to be a good daughter. But it always went back to the fire. Her fault.

And just like that, the guilt returned, clawing its way up her spine and around her throat, like ivy on steroids, choking the breath out of her.

You don't deserve a birthday party. Or anything else.

"Okay, now it's time for dinner." Connie swatted at Wade's shoulder. "Don't you make that face at me. I didn't cook it."

"Well, now I know what to give thanks for tomorrow." He smirked and ushered them into the dining room.

The meal was a delight. Connie wouldn't allow Susannah to move. Wade and Silver helped her carry in the many dishes of Chinese food and insisted everyone sample some of each.

"How did you know I was craving chicken balls?" Susannah asked, savoring the tangy sweet-and-sour sauce. "You'll have to roll me out of here."

"Not just yet." Connie beckoned to Darla and Silver who scurried into the kitchen with Wade behind.

"I wonder if I could talk to you later, Susannah," David murmured.

He was going to fire her. She knew it. He was so disgusted with her choice of the center for Darla, he was probably going to find someone else to do her job. Fierce, deep pain ripped through her.

Fool, he's not your friend. He's just a man who tolerated you because Darla liked you. You should have expected this. It's what you deserve.

"Fine. Later," she answered. There was no time to say anything else because an enormous cake appeared in the doorway, candles glowing merrily. Four voices broke out in song. "Thank you," she said when they were finished. "Thank you very much." And she meant it.

"Cut it, Susannah. I want to taste it." Darla wiggled on her chair. "I love cake!"

"Me, too," she said.

Who threw Darla's birthday party? David? The errant thought made Susannah pause before she slid the knife into the cake as she tried to picture what kind of party he would give her, what sort of cake they'd get her...

And then she remembered it was none of her business anymore.

David sat in the corner, sipped his coffee and paid little attention to the game he was supposed to be playing. All he could think about was how beautiful Susannah was, how she glowed in the soft lamplight of the family room.

She kept twiddling with her hair, trying to decide her next move. As a result, more and more tendrils had tumbled free and now curled around her long, slim neck. Her skin gleamed with the same porcelain translucence as the old master's paintings he'd seen in museums. Every so often she laid a delicate palm over her stomach and a funny, tender smile caressed her lips.

Once she'd caught him staring and turned an intense peach shade, the color of an Easter sunrise. David quickly looked away, pretending to concentrate on the task at hand.

Pointless. The mental image would not leave him.

"You won, Susannah!"

"I did?" She stared at Connie as if she couldn't imagine winning anything.

And once more David was reminded of her words, of her inability to grasp her own worth.

"Let's play charades now," Darla crowed.

David rose and left her to explain her favorite game. He wandered out to the back patio, studied the gleam of the water in the moon's bright light and tried to think about something other than Susannah Wells.

"You wanted to talk to me?" She stood behind him, her small body tense, her face a mask of no emotion.

"Will you sit down?"

"I'd rather walk a bit, if you don't mind?" She tried to smile and failed.

"Sure." David waited while she lifted the latch on the back gate. He held it open for her, breathing in her scent as she walked past.

"I eat so much and I don't get enough exercise. I'm going to have to go on a serious diet after the ba—" She cut herself off and said no more.

"I think you look beautiful."

"You do?" She'd been walking fast, trying to put some distance between them. But suddenly she stopped, turned and stared at him. "Me?"

"Pregnancy only enhances your beauty." He was surprised by how much he wanted her to believe him.

"Oh. Well, thank you." She stood there, a tiny furrow marring the perfection of her forehead. Then she shivered.

He slid off his jacket and laid it over her shoulders, watching her snuggle into the warmth as they walked down the street. "We won't stay out long. I'll just say my piece and go."

Susannah didn't say anything. But her wide green eyes darkened to the murky tones of the deep forest at dusk.

"I would like to apologize, Susannah."

"What?" She stared at him, shock swelling her pupils.

"I should never have said what I did at the center. I was way out of line." Shame filled David all over again. "Here I am, telling some woman in church to have a little Christian charity for Connie's work and I don't walk my talk. I've been worse than anyone for judging people and I'm sorry you had to hear that." He handed her an envelope. "This contains Darla's fee, and yours, for the pottery class."

"But—" Susannah's fine golden eyebrows rose. "I don't know how to do pottery."

He shrugged. "Use the money for whatever you feel is right. But please accept my apology for what I said."

"It doesn't matter." She turned and began walking toward Connie's home.

"Yes, Susannah, it does. It matters a lot that I hurt you." He caught her arm and coaxed her to stop so he could look into her eyes. "I know you're doing your best for Darla, and I appreciate it. There is no one else I'd feel as comfortable having with her as you, and I will never, ever question your judgment again. I promise."

She stared at him for a long time. Finally a tiny grin appeared.

"Ever? We'll see," she teased. Then her green eyes tipped down to his hand. Somehow he'd slid it down her arm until his fingers meshed with hers.

As if they were…good friends.

"They're not bad, you know." She whispered her plea for him to understand. "People won't give them a chance because they made some mistakes, but they're trying. Oliver hasn't had an easy life, but he's working it through."

"I know." He nodded. "And you're helping. I admire that."

"You do?" Susannah looked dumbfounded at first. Then she looked embarrassed. "I don't do anything."

"Give yourself some credit, will you?" he said. "Because of you, their paths, like Darla's, are a little easier. You take the time to find out what's bothering them, and then you put it right. That matters."

She didn't argue. She simply stood in place and studied him as if he were some foreign substance newly arrived on planet earth.

"I envy you, Susannah. Do you know that?" It cost a lot to admit it, but then David owed her a lot. He took her chin and tilted her face up so he could look into those amazing eyes. "You seem to intrinsically know what to do to soothe people. That's a gift from God, a serious gift. There aren't a lot of people who leave you feeling better about yourself than when they arrived. But you do."

She lowered her eyelids, hiding her expression. But her smooth cheeks turned a pearly pink in the shadows of a streetlight and she drew her hand away from his.

"I think you would make an awesome mother to your baby. I don't think there would be a child on earth that could have a woman more determined to give her baby all the love it needs to make it through this world." He took both her forearms then and tugged so she would look at him. "Won't you reconsider this adoption thing, Susannah? Please?"

He held his breath, hoping. Praying.

"I can't." She drew away. "And I don't want to talk about this anymore. Connie might overhear." She frowned at him. "You promised."

"I won't break my word." He waited while she lifted the hook on the gate, and then followed her through. "But I wish you'd reconsider."

Susannah closed the gate. She slid his jacket off her shoulders and handed it to him. Her small pointed chin lifted in determination.

"It would never work." Her face closed up tight, the radiance that had lit her from the inside dimmed, quashed by some fear he couldn't see.

"Susannah—"

She shook her head.

"I'm not who you think I am, David."

"I don't think you are who you think you are, either," he replied. "Nor do I think you have any idea of what you could become."

She gazed at him for a moment longer, then walked into the house.

His heart pinched at the sadness of it. Susannah wouldn't let herself consider keeping her child. Wouldn't believe in herself that much. And he wasn't exactly sure

why, except that the problem was rooted in her past—
rooted firmly.

But what could he do?

Instead of returning inside he sat down beside the pool
to think. As usual, images of Susannah filled his mind.
He saw again that tender, bemused smile flickering over
her face, the bewildered yet amazed way she touched her
midsection.

A baby, a tiny, innocent child. A son. Or a daughter
to whom she would give life and upon whom she could
pour out the love she gave so freely to others.

Darla had told him Susannah had begun to talk about
her child, and had mentioned how Susannah often offered
to hold other women's children at the center.

To give up her child would leave a scar. One that
would wound far deeper than the pain sweet Susannah
now carried from her past.

And that was something David could not even con-
template, let alone allow. To see this beautiful woman
retreat back to the scared, sad person who'd arrived here
only a few months ago tore at his heart.

Don't get involved, his head reminded.

Only David knew it wasn't a matter of involvement
now. Susannah had breached his defenses, pushed her
way past all his intentions to remain aloof, and invei-
gled herself into his world through Darla. Susannah had
become part of his days, sneaked into his dreams and
made his heart wish for things he couldn't have.

It was silly, impossible to think of a future with her.
His brain had long since accepted that God's choice for
his life's path didn't lie that way. He had responsibilities. Love wasn't for him. Hadn't he learned that lesson
twice? If only that lesson would sink into the secret parts

of him that longed to experience being a husband and a father.

But that silly longing for something he couldn't have didn't mean he should give up trying to persuade Susannah that adoption was not the way to go.

All David had to figure out was how to do that.

He'd start with money. A little nest egg for her baby. Maybe if she felt she had something to fall back on, that she wasn't teetering on the brink—maybe then Susannah wouldn't feel so compelled to give up her child for adoption.

Maybe.

Chapter Ten

Susannah felt only relief when Thanksgiving and Christmas slid past in a rush that left her little time to think.

Pregnancy was a confusing business and no one was more confused than she. Especially with the increased fluttering her baby now made.

Her baby.

She had to stop thinking of it that way. It could never be hers.

On New Year's, Susannah decided to make plans for her future and wrote lists of actions she needed to take. But in the days following, she rewrote them over and over, depending on where her moods took her.

Those moods took her a lot of places. Into the pool late at night when she couldn't sleep. To the ice cream shop to taste weird flavors. To a crochet class at the center where she struggled to make a baby blanket the instructor insisted was "simple."

When no answer from her mother arrived to respond to the plea for forgiveness she'd sent earlier, Susannah found herself weepy and tearful, unable to accept Connie's assurance that God loved her. How could God love someone who'd made the mistakes she had? Her mother sure didn't love her. Susannah couldn't even love herself.

But she loved her baby. She loved that life inside her with every ounce of passion in her body. She would do anything, anything to protect it, including finding new parents for her baby—if only she could.

But that wasn't her only problem. Susannah was growing fearful of her burgeoning feelings for David Foster. Especially since he'd become so thoughtful, so—nice. But though she enjoyed being around him, enjoyed the way he made her feel part of his and Darla's world—Susannah would not let those feelings grow. She couldn't. She couldn't afford a repeat mistake—not with this baby's future at stake.

So Susannah was confused, wary and seven months pregnant when she arrived at David's office late one January morning. Thus far they'd always talked when he came home at the end of the day. But today he'd asked her to come to his office.

As she entered the exquisitely appointed building, she was enthralled by a granite wall down which water trickled. In contrast to the Tucson desert, lush plants thrived all around it with light from the massive windows. The office felt grand—and she felt totally out of place.

"Hello, Susannah. Welcome." David escorted her to his office, his hand firm but gentle against her back.

"It's beautiful in here," she whispered.

"Thank you." He seated her in a cranberry velvet chair that folded around her weary body, and then asked his secretary to bring them tea.

The girl flirted with David, batting her long lashes, making sure to bend over in front of him when she set down the tea and sumptuous-looking lemon and poppy seed muffins. Susannah disliked the secretary immediately and she refused both tea and muffins, though her stomach grumbled a complaint.

"I'd rather have coffee," she said when David held out a steaming white china cup that probably cost the earth.

"You're supposed to cut down on coffee, aren't you?" He set the cup in front of her, undaunted by her glower.

"Who told you that?" she demanded, then sighed. "Darla."

"She loves to talk about you and your baby. And I like to hear," he added.

"You do?" That shocked her. "Why?"

"Who doesn't like to hear about a new life preparing to join our world?" One brown eyebrow lifted. "It's generous of you to share the details of your pregnancy with her." He leaned back in his chair as he sipped his tea. "I imagine it's quite amazing to have a life growing inside you."

"It is," she admitted. Susannah tilted her head down to hide her smile of pure delight. It was astonishing, in fact. But she felt embarrassed to tell him that. Especially here, where she was so out of place.

She hoped the coffee table hid her feet as she slipped off her shoes. Even they didn't seem to fit anymore.

"You're probably wondering why I asked you here." His voice changed from gentle concern to businesslike.

"Yes." In fact, curiosity was eating her up.

"I've done quite a bit of research into adoptions." He caught her surprise. "I had to," he explained. "It's not exactly my field."

"Oh." So she'd put him to a lot of trouble. How much would all that cost? He kept telling her not to worry about the cost, but she did worry.

"The thing is, Susannah, I need some direction. There are so many kinds of adoptions. I'm not sure which you prefer." He handed her a file filled with papers. "These describe open and closed adoptions and what choices, responsibilities and rights the mother had in specific cases."

"Okay." She set the sheaf down on the glass table. She'd think about it later. She picked up her teacup. Suddenly she was very thirsty.

"There are many variations," he continued. "For instance, do you want contact with your baby after you give it away?"

He made her baby sound like a used toy she was getting rid of.

"I don't know," Susannah murmured.

"Do you want to be involved in raising your child or are you intending to hand over all rights to the child's future and give the adoptive parents total freedom?" David leaned back in his chair and studied her.

"I don't—"

"Will you want the adoptive parents to tell the child about you or do you prefer your baby never know its real mother?"

"Uh—" Susannah frowned.

Never know anything about her? Never know that she loved her child desperately, that she yearned to keep it for her very own, to shower on it all the love she kept hidden inside? An arrow of pain pierced her heart. She laid a protective hand on her stomach.

"I—I'm not sure about that yet," she whispered.

"Will you release medical records?" he asked.

"I don't know." So many questions. She was growing more confused.

"Grandparents?"

"No!" At least she knew the answer to that question. Her hand squeezed tight against her purse where the condemning letter lay. "Never."

"You don't want the child to be able to trace his family roots someday?" David asked, his face puzzled.

"My father left when I was four. I doubt even I could trace his whereabouts," she told him, her body clenching with tension.

"What about your mother? Wouldn't she—"

"She's in prison." She watched his eyes, steeling herself to see disgust. But David never flinched.

"Do you ever see her?" he asked.

"She doesn't want to see me." Susannah's cheeks burned. She picked up her cup again and sipped just to have something to do with her hands. "She hates me."

"I see." Those dark eyes pinned her down, as if she was a witness on the stand. "So no family history. That's what you want for your child?"

Susannah almost gagged.

"It will be better that way," she blurted. "It's what I have to do."

"Actually you don't. That's what I'm trying to clarify," he said, leaning forward so his elbows were on his knees. "You have choices, Susannah. Lots of them. Your child is yours. You make the decisions. I'll do whatever you want."

"Okay." She nodded.

"But I have to be certain you understand what you're doing," he said, his voice solemn. "I would be failing you as your lawyer if later you regretted your decision."

"Let's not go over that again," she said, rising. She stepped away from the coffee table, searching with her feet for her shoes. But as she tried to slip her foot into one, she lost her balance and reached out to grab something to steady herself.

That something was him.

"Easy." His arm slid around her waist. "Sit down and I'll put them on for you."

"I can manage." She drew back and wished she hadn't. Her head whirled. Being this near to him made her want all kinds of things—like someone to care about her, someone to love her.

Stupid. David Foster wasn't interested in her. He was just being nice.

"Do you ever let someone help you without an argument?" His mouth tipped in a crooked grin. With gentleness and great care, he helped her sit. Then he knelt down in front of her to slide on her sandals. "You should put your feet up," he murmured, brushing his fingers against her calf. "Your ankles are swollen."

"All of me is swollen. I look like a truck."

David chuckled. Susannah burst into tears.

"Stop laughing at me!"

"I'm not laughing at you." Somehow he was there beside her, holding her close, allowing her to weep all over his expensive suit jacket. "I'm laughing at the way you mistake things. You are beautiful, Susannah, one of the most beautiful women I've ever known. Motherhood has only made you more beautiful."

"I can never be a mother." Grief swamped her.

"Talk to me, Susannah." David cupped her face in his hand. "Tell me what this is really about," he said in a soft, tender voice. "Tell me the whole story."

The burden was so heavy. And Susannah was so tired.

The words emerged of their own volition. She stared into his concerned face and let it pour out of her.

"I was the oldest. I promised my sisters I'd always be there for them. They were only four and seven. Little girls who needed someone to watch out for them. But I didn't do that. I ran away." Loathing scathed her voice. "They died because of me."

"No." He seemed dazed, incredulous.

She smiled bitterly. "Believe it. They're dead."

"You said there was a fire," he said. "How could that be your fault?"

"Easy." She pulled out of his hold and gathered her courage. When he knew, he would send her away. Might as well just get it over with. "I wanted to get away from the chaos. I was so tired of having to figure out what was for dinner, what we were supposed to wear to school, how we were going to pay the electric bill. Scared of being scared all the time."

She'd never told anyone that, not even Connie.

"Those are things your mother should have handled."

"She couldn't, so I did." Tears glossed her eyes, but she refused to shed them. She forced herself to continue. "My sisters died because of me, David. It was my fault. I killed them."

Give me words, Lord, because I don't have any, David prayed silently. His heart ached to ease the inner torment her eyes revealed.

"Susannah—"

"Now do you understand why I cannot—I will not—raise this child?"

David studied the weeping woman in front of him. He doubted Susannah even realized that she was cradling her baby as she spoke. He couldn't begin to imagine how one small woman could bear so much pain.

"Why don't you say anything? Are you disgusted? Revolted?" she asked, anger sparking her eyes. "Well, so am I. And I will never let a child of mine feel that way."

Help her!

"Susannah, how old were you when they died?"

"Nine. I was their big sister. S'ana they used to call me when they hugged me at night." A flicker of a smile appeared and vanished. "I tried so hard to keep them safe."

"Of course you did," he whispered, smoothing damp curls from her brow. "You protected them and loved them as much or more than your mom did, didn't you? You would have done anything for them."

She stared at him, nodding in a dazed manner as if she'd never thought of it in those terms.

"You were a great big sister, Susannah. But doesn't it seem to you, now that you're older and can look back, that nine was far too young to be responsible for two other children?" David held his breath as she frowned, tilted her head to one side.

"I was responsible," she repeated, confusion evident.

"You weren't, sweetheart. You were not their mother."

She simply looked at him.

"Your mother was there, right?" He waited for her nod. "She was in the house when you left?"

"Yes."

"Doing what?" He had to get to the bottom of it, had to make her see.

Susannah was quiet for a long time. Finally she lifted her eyes and looked at him. "She was drunk. She was often drunk."

He touched her cheek. "But that didn't make it your

job to do any of those things you said, Susannah. It was only your job to love your sisters, and it sounds to me like you did. Very much. Enough to take care of them the very best you could. All by yourself."

"You make me sound like some kind of hero," she protested. "I wasn't. I left them. I ran away."

"What nine-year-old doesn't run away from home at least once? I did." He took her hand in his, marveling at the coldness of it. Such a small, frail hand, a frail body to house such a big heart. "Maybe you shouldn't have sneaked out, but that does not make you responsible for their deaths."

"Legally, you mean." Was that hope dawning?

"I mean you were not responsible in any way, shape or form. Not legally and not morally," David insisted. "You were a child, as your sisters were. The guilty person was your mother, Susannah."

"No." She shook her head with determination. "She couldn't help it. When my dad walked out she was so hurt. She was always crying."

"So she got drunk to dull the pain?"

"I guess so." Susannah blinked away the tears. "She fell asleep that day and…it wasn't her fault. I should have been there." She shrugged dully. "It doesn't matter anymore."

"Yes, it does." David had to make her see it. "It matters a lot. You cut your mother plenty of slack, but you can't do that for yourself?"

"I don't deserve it."

"Why don't you? You were a child." He swallowed hard, then spoke the words he knew in his heart were true. "She told you it was your fault, didn't she? Your mom blamed you?"

"Yes," Susannah whispered. "But she was right—"

"She was wrong," he said, his anger burning white-hot. "So wrong."

"No." Susannah shook her head. "She was in pain. She didn't know, didn't realize that I wasn't there—"

"But she should have, don't you see? She was the one who was responsible for taking care of the three of you and she dumped that duty on you, a young child." He could hardly speak, so infuriated was he at this woman who had so wounded her own grieving child.

"She must have thought I was home to watch them," she murmured.

"You told her you were leaving?"

"Yes, but I didn't make sure she heard. I wanted to escape." Susannah lifted her head and stared at him through her tears. "Why did God let my sisters die? Why didn't He let me die instead?"

"Oh, Susannah." He gathered her into his arms and held her tightly, trying to ease the burden of her loss. "God doesn't want you to die. He wants you to live and make something wonderful out of your life. And you're doing it."

"I am?" She lifted her head, her face inches from his, hope flickering.

It was all David could do not to kiss her. But he held back because he understood that now more than ever, Susannah needed to know about the kind of love that would always be there for her.

"Of course you are." He smoothed the tendrils off her face. "God has given you this opportunity and you're doing your best to make good."

"How?" she asked, forehead furrowed.

"You're making sure your baby has a good start, for one thing. You're eating right and exercising. You're seeing your doctor regularly, right?" He didn't like the way her gaze skewed away from his. "Aren't you?"

"I will go again, as soon as I can pay," she whispered.

"What? No, Susannah." David shook his head. He tilted her chin so she had to look at him. "You don't have to pay. Didn't the doctor's office tell you that?"

"No." She leaned back to look at him, her face troubled. "Why wouldn't I pay?"

"Because you have insurance. I bought it for you." He liked the way she fit in his arms—liked it a lot. "All of my employees have health insurance."

"Oh." A soft glow flickered through her eyes. "Does it cover sonograms?"

"It covers whatever you need," David said. He wanted to keep holding her, keep reassuring her. He wanted more. He wanted…everything.

The realization shocked him.

And terrified him.

He couldn't have love, or marriage and a family. The things other men took for granted—a wife, family—God had not chosen for him. He knew that.

So why this irrational need to protect Susannah, to make sure she was cared for, that her child was not given away to strangers?

"I had a sonogram a while ago," she was saying. "I was supposed to have another one, but I didn't have quite enough money saved." She explained that she'd paid for the first one.

David needed distance between them to calm his racing heart. He eased her out of his arms as he made a mental note to claim Susannah's money back.

"Make the appointment and have the test done immediately," he insisted. "If you need another doctor, special treatment, anything—I'll make sure it's covered. We want this baby healthy. Don't we?"

"Yes." She struggled to rise.

He rushed to help her, realizing anew how difficult her pregnancy was making things.

"Susannah, I want you to know something."

"What?" She peered at him warily.

"I've put away some money for you. In case you change your mind about the baby." He put one finger on her lips to stop her protest. "I don't want you to feel that adoption is your only option. If you want to keep your baby, you can do it." He slid the bankbook from his pocket and into her hand.

"You shouldn't have done this, David." She opened it and blanched at the amount, going even whiter than she was before. "This is wrong."

"I pay into a pension plan for my staff," he said quietly. "Think of that as your pension plan." When she still frowned, he folded her fingers around it. "I won't take it back. It's yours, to help however you want."

"It's unbelievable." Susannah was silent for several moments. Then she looked at him, her eyes glossy with unshed tears, and nodded. "I don't know how to thank you."

"You don't have to." He frowned at her pallor. "Are you certain you're all right to look after Darla? You're not overdoing it?"

"I'm fine. I shouldn't say this but it's a really easy job." She smiled. "Darla has changed a lot, hasn't she?"

"Thanks to you." He smiled at her, loving the way she glowed with pride whenever she spoke about his sister. "You've done a great job."

She lowered her gaze, shy as always when compliments came her way. His anger flared again at the mother who'd treated her so shabbily.

"I better go." She walked toward the door and paused. "Oh, one other thing." She fiddled with the strap on her handbag. "Darla wants to work as a junior assistant at the butterfly exhibit at the botanical garden. We've visited frequently and the director thinks she has a knack for speaking to the kids who visit."

"When? Her schedule already seems pretty full," David mused.

"It is," Susannah agreed. "But I think she can do this. I think she needs to do it, David. She needs the confidence this public responsibility will give her. Isn't that what we've been trying to achieve?"

He liked the "we" part of what Susannah said. But Darla on show in a public place? It was something he'd secretly avoided ever since her accident.

"She isn't the same girl, David. She's learned how to manage her feelings. This can only help her gain further control." Susannah's quiet plea reached into his heart and touched a chord there. "Darla needs to feel needed. This is her chance to prove to herself that she has a place in the world."

David hesitated. He didn't like it, would never have countenanced it if Susannah hadn't pushed. But so far she had been right about his sister.

"Are you going to be there?" How had he and Darla managed before Susannah's arrival?

"Of course. For the first time or two, anyway. Just in case she needs me." Susannah smiled at him. "She can do it?"

"Okay."

"Great!" She raced across the floor and threw her arms around him in a burst of exuberance. "Thank you," she said, hugging him. Then she stepped back, cheeks hot pink as her arms dropped to her side. "Sorry."

"No problem." David grinned. She was truly the most beautiful woman—inside and out—that he'd ever known. "I enjoyed it."

That made her cheeks even pinker. David enjoyed seeing her so flustered.

"When is her first day?" he asked. "I'd like to visit."

"Probably Saturday." She checked her watch. "I have to go. Thank you, David, for everything." She started for the door.

"Susannah?"

"Yes?" She stopped and turned.

"Take these and read them." He picked up the sheaf of papers from the table and offered them to her. "Will you please think about what I said, about keeping your baby?"

She took the papers but shook her head.

"Why not?"

"It's better if my baby has a new mother." Then she hurried away.

It wasn't better at all, David fumed. It was wrong. Totally wrong that Susannah of the loving heart should give up her child. What kind of a mother had she lived with to skew her thinking so much?

He decided to find out. He sat down at his desk, picked up the phone and asked his research assistant to dig up everything on Susannah's mother.

"There has to be a way, Lord. You surely couldn't want Susannah to give up this gift You've given her."

Why do I care?

Because I love her.

The admittance knocked him sideways. It shouldn't

have—he quickly realized that he'd been carrying strong feelings for Susannah for a long time.

She was gentle, loving and tender. She'd made a ton of mistakes and she knew it. Which meant she carried a boatload of guilt from her past.

None of which mattered one iota to him.

Susannah loved Darla. She'd gone beyond what any caregiver could be expected to do to help his sister figure out her world. David would have loved her for that alone. But he loved her for so much more.

He loved her because she didn't let him get away with anything, because she listened—really listened—to him, because she never once, in all these months, had asked for anything for herself. Yet he wanted to give her everything.

And because of that, David wanted—no, needed—to make it possible for Susannah to keep her baby.

He picked up the phone.

"Wade? Can you and Jared meet me tomorrow for lunch? I really need to talk to you guys. Thanks."

They were his best friends, they knew his history and most important of all, they shared his faith. David had no clear-cut answer from God on what to do with his feelings but they could help him figure out his next step.

Love was something that wasn't for him. He knew that.

Yet love was exactly what he felt for Susannah Wells.

So what was he supposed to do?

Chapter Eleven

"So you've fallen in love with Susannah," Wade said and clapped him on the shoulder. "Congratulations."

"It's not that simple," David said.

"Why?" Jared demanded. "What's wrong with love?"

"It's not for me, that's what. It's not part of God's plan for me." David rose and paced around Wade's patio. But that silence got to him. He looked up and caught the puzzled look his buddies were sharing. "I've been engaged before," he reminded them.

"So?" Jared shrugged. "They weren't the right ones. Susannah is."

"But how can I be sure of that?"

"Dave, sit down and let's work this through. You care about Susannah, right?" Wade asked after he'd flopped onto one of the chairs beside the pool.

"Yes."

"Okay." Wade nodded. "And you want her and her baby in your life permanently?"

"Yes," he repeated with certainty.

"But you think that's somehow wrong?" Jared frowned. "Why?"

"Because I'm not good husband material. I have Darla

to care for, I work long hours." He glared at them. "Two other women walked away from me."

"Yes, we know. And if they'd been God's choice, don't you think He would have sent one of them back?" Jared rested his elbows on his knees. "I'm no expert on love, but I've read the Bible and I can't find a place where it says you have no right to love. In fact, God is love. He patterns love for us. He doesn't place love in your heart and then demand that you ignore it. Where does it say that in the Bible, David?"

"I agree. If that's your thinking, you ought to be able to line it up against His word. Chapter and verse, buddy." Wade leaned back, waiting.

"Of course there's no verse," David said, irritated that they kept pushing. "It's just something I know."

"How do you know it?" Jared demanded. "Because you were thrown over twice? That's not proof that you can't have love in your life, that you can't love someone."

"There's one thing I've learned about love this past year, David." Wade's voice dropped but remained intense. "God gives us love to enrich our lives, so we can share with someone who will be there for us, help us through the good stuff and the bad stuff. It seems to me that's what you have going with Susannah. And I think it's wonderful. What I don't get is why you can't accept a gift like that from your heavenly Father."

"It's just—I don't believe He meant that kind of relationship for me." David didn't know how else to express it.

"Exactly. *You* don't believe. You." Jared glanced at Wade who nodded and began speaking again.

"Listen, buddy. Jared and I think that this so-called truth of yours, that God doesn't want you to love, is something you've convinced yourself of. I know being dumped the second time, especially when she blamed Darla for your failing relationship, had to be hard on your ego." Wade winced. "When my first wife took off with some other guy, I felt gutted. I couldn't even imagine I'd be able to care for another woman, let alone love one again. I made up my mind that I would never get involved again. But God brought Connie into my life."

"And now look at him," Jared teased. "Seriously, though, just because Wade thought and felt like that didn't make it God's plan for him, Dave. It's the same with you. You wanted to avoid the hurt and embarrassment those fiancées brought you. That's understandable. But you don't care for either of them now, do you?"

"No." David was emphatic on that. The only woman in his heart now was Susannah.

"Because you love Susannah," Wade said.

"Yes." It felt so good to admit that aloud.

"There's nothing wrong with that," Jared insisted. "Love is God-given. You might also tell Susannah how you feel. Maybe she feels the same?"

How David wished that were true.

"But if you're still doubting," Jared said, "why don't you pray about it and ask God to work it out for you? If she's the one, don't you think God had a hand in bringing you two together? Don't you think He has a plan to make it all work out?"

"Is it God you don't trust, David?" Wade asked. "Or is it yourself?"

"Hello, baby."

Susannah blinked through her tears at the shadowy image of her child on the sonogram picture the technician had given her. With her fingertip she traced the tiny head, the neck, two perfect arms and legs—her baby. The wonder of this life growing inside her blindsided her to everything else.

So tiny. So precious.

How could she let this child go?

How could I not?

Her baby would soon be born and she'd have to hand him or her over to strangers. Forever.

Susannah's heartache intensified as the desolating loss swamped her. Though she tried to suppress them, tears flowed in a steady stream down her cheeks.

If only David was right, if only she could keep her child. What a sweet and generous gesture to give her the money. Susannah's Baby, he'd written on the bankbook. Once again she marveled at his generosity and the way he saw beyond what everyone else did, probing to the heart of things. He figured out she didn't have anything and went the extra mile to ensure she could make her choice with no regret.

But it wasn't about the money, never had been. It was about her inability to handle such a massive responsibility without messing up. And so she decided that when she left Tucson she'd make sure he got his money back.

Susannah stared down at the picture again and new tears flowed. She was glad Darla was outside playing with Silver. She didn't want anyone to witness her weakness. Because it was weak to want what you couldn't have, what you knew you'd ruin.

"Susannah?" David stood before her. "What's wrong?"

He crouched down to study the paper in her hand. She watched him examine the image, a huge smile spreading across his face from one side to the other. Delight lit his eyes as he examined the picture in minute detail. Finally he lifted his gaze to meet hers.

"Your baby," he whispered. "It's perfect, Susannah. Is it a boy or a girl?"

"I didn't ask." She dashed the tears away. "I only asked if it was healthy," she said. The words dissolved into a blubber as her emotions seesawed again.

"And?" he asked, sitting beside her. Somehow she was in his arms again, and she didn't mind one bit.

"It is." She sighed as he gathered her close and let her rest against him. She was so tired. "The doctor says everything is great."

"Good. Then we should celebrate this gift of life God's given you. Not cry about it." His hand smoothed over her back in a soothing caress that made her feel loved, cherished, cared for.

"Celebrate?" She leaned back. "How?"

David chuckled as he brushed her cheek with his knuckles, drying her tears. He gently released her before smoothing the long strands of hair she'd left free. Susannah felt the faintest caress of his lips against her forehead before he rose.

"I'm not sure how," he said, staring at her. "But this healthy baby definitely deserves a pre-birthday celebration."

"Can we have a party, Davy?" Darla said from the doorway. "Silver is staying for dinner."

"I hope you have a lovely time," Susannah murmured, too tired to get up. Everything seemed to suck her energy these days. "I think I'll go home."

"Connie and Wade went out for dinner, didn't they? So you haven't eaten. I could order in a pizza," David offered.

"No." Darla shook her head at him. "No pizza."

"I thought you liked pizza," he said, obviously bewildered.

"I do. But Susannah's baby doesn't like it." Darla moved to sit beside Susannah. She put her hand on her stomach and gently stroked. "It kicks her and upsets her stomach when she eats pizza. Then she can't sleep, and Susannah needs to sleep lots." She frowned at her big brother. "We have to have something else."

What a girl. Susannah smiled at her protector, glad she wouldn't be forced to eat the spicy Italian food she usually loved.

"Okay. What would you prefer, Susannah? I'm guessing sushi is out?"

She made a face.

"That's what I thought." He grinned. "Is that because you can't put peanut butter on sushi?"

"Ew, gross." Darla made a gagging motion.

"You don't have to order anything for me, but I'm sure the girls would love cheeseburgers," Susannah said, trying to get the focus off of herself.

"Too greasy. I think stir-fried vegetables would be good." Darla glanced at her friend. "We like Chinese food, don't we, Silver?"

"We like it lots," Silver agreed, grinning. "Especially me."

"Good. Chinese it is. How about if you two come with me to pick it up. Then Susannah can have a rest." David bent over Susannah, his nose a centimeter from hers. "And I do mean rest. Put your feet up and have a nap. No setting the table or anything else."

"It sounds lovely," she agreed, enjoying the way he slipped off her shoes and playfully placed them across the room. "Thank you."

"You're welcome." His toffee-toned eyes held hers for a moment.

It had been a very warm day, but Darla insisted on covering her with an afghan before they left. She tucked it around Susannah's feet, her face brimming with concern.

"You won't get up?" she asked anxiously.

"I promise." Susannah waved as they left. She'd intended to watch a documentary about childbirth, but somehow her brain began replaying that moment when David had kissed her forehead. She fell to dreaming about what it would be like to be cared for, loved, by a man like him, a man who wouldn't dump you the moment life took a wrong turn.

A man who would cherish you and protect you and make life fun again.

A man who would love a baby that wasn't even his.

"Davy, can you help me?"

"Sure, sis. With what?"

"Susannah." Darla frowned. "Me and Silver are worried about her."

"You are? Why?" He'd been a little worried himself when he'd found her weeping like that. "I think she was crying because she was so happy to see that picture of her baby," he said.

"I don't mean that." Darla shook her head. "Susannah gets really tired. Silver heard her tell Connie that the baby is moving around a lot and she can't sleep. One night Silver saw her swimming and it was really late."

"I think that's the way it is with babies," he said, wondering where she was going with this. "I think Susannah is okay though, Darla."

"But Connie said the doctor told Susannah to slow

down, to stop trying to do so much, and she doesn't. Susannah thinks she has to do everything with me. It's my fault she gets so tired." She glanced at Silver who was playing at the juke box, then leaned closer. "Maybe if she didn't get so tired all the time, Susannah wouldn't want to give away her baby," she whispered.

"Sweetie, she doesn't want to give it away, exactly. She's just afraid she won't be able to look after it," he explained.

"She won't if she's too tired," Darla said. "We could adopt it. I would help."

"I know you would, sweetie," David said. He touched her hand. "But I don't think Susannah wants that."

"I guess not. We're not a family and Susannah wants a family." Darla sighed.

"Listen kid, you and I are a family. Always have been, always will be. Got it?" He bussed her cheek with his fist.

"Yeah, but we're not the kind of family that can take care of a baby, are we, Davy?"

He shook his head, unsure of how to deny that. So far he'd been focused on the two of them, not on including anyone else, though he'd wanted exactly that for years.

"Could you come with us to the botanical garden tomorrow?" Darla said. "Susannah says she has to be there, but it's hot in the butterfly exhibit and she might get too tired. She could go and rest if you were there."

"I have an appointment tomorrow afternoon. I was going to come after that," he told her.

"Could you put it off? Or send somebody else?" Darla asked anxiously. "We have to help Susannah now. 'Cause we love her."

Yes, we do, he thought.

"Okay, I'll do my best," he promised.

"And can we get a chair and an umbrella for soccer?" she asked. "There are only hard benches there and there's no shade."

"I'll figure something out, sweetie." He hugged her, touched by her compassion. "You just tell me when you see something we can do to help, and I'll do it."

"Well, we were talking about that," she said, waving at Silver to come over. "Tell him," she ordered.

"Susannah likes flowers." Having abandoned the juke box, Silver flopped down on a stool. "She told me nobody ever gave her flowers before. My dad gives Connie flowers lots of times."

"Hmm. How about if we pick up some flowers on the way home." David made a mental note to make sure Susannah got lots of flowers. Such a small thing. How sad that no one had been there to do that for her. He intended to change that.

Their food arrived and David carried it out to the car. On the way home he pulled into a flower shop and let the girls choose a bouquet for Susannah—a bright spring one. He also spotted a portable chair with a little umbrella attached.

"Perfect," Darla told him with a grin.

Satisfied, David drove home—and found Susannah sleeping on the sofa.

"She really is Sleeping Beauty," Darla whispered.

"No, I'm not. I'm a troll who needs her dinner. Grr," Susannah said, eyes closed. She grinned at them as she eased upright.

David extended a hand to help her to her feet, marveling at the difference a little sleep made. Her green eyes shone with life, her skin luminous.

"Feeling better?" he asked as they laid the table.

"Much." She blushed when he held out her chair for her and quickly sat. "Thanks."

"You're welcome." He couldn't resist touching the swath of golden curls that cascaded down her back.

"These are for you, from us." Darla held out the bouquet with pride.

"Oh. Thank you." Susannah glanced at him, startled. Then she accepted the flowers and buried her nose in the fragrant petals. "They're beautiful."

David could have sworn he saw tears in her eyes, but when she looked at the girls, she'd blinked them away and was smiling. He got a vase, filled it with water and set it in the middle of the table so she could enjoy her bouquet.

"Only two months till Easter," he said, holding up his water glass to toast her. "Not long to go now."

"That's easy for you to say. I have a quite different perspective." She peeked through her eyelashes, grinning.

And David lost his breath. She actually sounded happy about the future.

"I'm starving," Darla said.

"Me, two," Susannah agreed and winked at Silver.

"Me, three." Silver giggled.

They all looked at him with expectant eyes.

"Me, four?" Susannah burst into laughter.

"Say grace, Davy."

David offered a quick prayer of thanks then served everyone, enjoying the pleasure of making sure each had enough to eat. It had been a long time since a meal around this kitchen table had been so happy and he knew it had everything to do with Susannah's presence. He couldn't stop staring at her.

David felt compelled to study Susannah's radiant face as the girls teased her about her appetite. This afternoon

Wade and Jared had helped David realize that he wanted this woman and her child in his life permanently. His friends had insisted there was no reason why David couldn't care for Susannah, that cutting love out of his life had never been something God had told him. Repeatedly they'd asked him to show a Biblical foundation for his belief that love was wrong for him. Wade had even said he thought David had made himself believe that after being thrown over twice.

But were they right?

And how risky was it to love her?

Susannah wasn't like David's former fiancées. He didn't have to wonder if she'd walk out because he worked too long, or because of something Darla did. Susannah knew what his life was like, knew he was committed to his sister. She was committed, too.

But could she love him?

"You're not eating," she said, frowning at him. "Is something wrong?"

"No." He felt the worries, the cares, the heavy thoughts go as he returned her smile. "Nothing is wrong at all."

Life seemed so simple, so enjoyable when Susannah was there.

"I'll help clean up," she offered when the food had disappeared.

"There isn't much to clean up." David chuckled at the one lonely chicken ball rolling in sauce. "I can load everything into the dishwasher. You go and rest."

"I did rest," she told him, a glimmer of spirit flickering in her gorgeous eyes. "And I'm fine. Perfectly able to clean up a few dishes. So don't argue," she added when he opened his mouth.

"Okay. You can help a little," he agreed, pretending he'd made the decision.

David enjoyed the camaraderie of working beside Susannah. He made a big fuss about giving her plenty of room for the sheer pleasure of watching her blush.

He drove back to Connie and Wade's enjoying the sound of laughter and happy voices. Darla raced out of the car and up the walk with Silver, leaving him and Susannah alone in the car.

"It was nice to have someone to share our table with," he said. "I'd forgotten how long it's been since Darla and I entertained."

"I hope you don't feel you have to entertain me," Susannah said, frowning at him. "I'm just the help."

"Susannah, you must know you mean a lot more than that to us," he said meaningfully. He held her gaze until she looked away.

"Thank you for these," she said, burying her nose in her flowers. "I've never had—well, thank you."

"You're welcome." David climbed out and went to open her car door. "What time will Darla be working at the butterfly exhibit tomorrow?"

"You're going to come?" She didn't look exactly thrilled at the prospect.

"I'll try to get there," he said. "I want to see how she does. Is that a problem?"

Susannah drew in a breath and stared past his shoulder. She wore a pained look that made him wonder if he'd said something wrong.

"Susannah? Are you all right?"

Finally she exhaled and nodded. "Yes."

"Did something just happen?" he asked as a wave of concern rushed over him. He grasped her elbow in case she felt faint or something. "You don't look pale."

She slid her arm out of his touch and smiled. "I can't get used to the soccer game going on inside me, that's all."

She let him escort her to the door before she hugged Darla and waved at him. "See you tomorrow." She inclined her head at Darla. "She'll be helping after school till five o'clock."

"Oh. Yes. Okay." David scanned her face once more. "You're sure you're all right?"

"I'm fine. Good night." She stood in the doorway, waiting for them to leave.

"Good night." He helped Darla into the car, and they drove away. Susannah remained in the doorway, her focus on the picture she clutched in her hands, the picture of her baby.

A wash of yearning swamped him. All down the block families were heading inside their homes, gathering their loved ones around them. David wanted to be able to do the same thing with Susannah. To protect her, to share her life, to have the right to help her with her child, and not just be an outsider.

He wanted to be able to kiss her good-night and wake up to her smiling face, to share his hopes and dreams with her, to discuss Darla and seek her opinion. He wanted Susannah to help him build a family.

God, please give me the sense to wait for the right time and find the words to tell her how much she means to me.

"I love Susannah, Davy," Darla said, yawning as she followed him inside their dark and silent home. "She makes everything happy."

"She sure does."

Darla stopped at the bottom of the stairs and frowned at him.

"What's wrong?" he asked.

"Susannah might come and stay with us forever if you kissed her like Prince Charming kissed Sleeping Beauty," she said. "Couldn't you kiss her, Davy?"

"We'll see," he said as he struggled to keep a straight face. "Have a good sleep, sweetie."

"Yeah." She hugged him, started up the stairs, then paused. "Davy?"

"Yes?" He waited, knowing something important was coming.

"Are you sure we couldn't adopt Susannah's baby?" Sadness drained the joy from her face. "I don't want that baby or Susannah to go away. I love them both."

"I know." David embraced her and tried to soothe her, but he couldn't tell her everything would be okay. Because he wasn't sure it would be—not for Susannah once she let her child go, and not for him if he let Susannah go.

"What can we do, Davy?"

"Pray," was the only answer he could think of.

Darla was doing an amazing job explaining the butterfly exhibit to the group of day-care children who were visiting the botanical garden. Susannah smiled encouragement when two older boys wandered in and began to ask Darla a hundred questions. Susannah listened but her mind was on finding somewhere to sit. She was so tired and the little butterfly gazebo was so hot.

Loud voices drew her attention.

Darla was supposed to inspect and brush off each person to ensure no butterflies hid in their clothes and escaped the enclosure. But the boys would not let her do it. In fact, they taunted her. Susannah stepped forward to intervene, but at that moment one of the boys jerked back and knocked her off balance. She reached out, desperate to grab on to a metal fountain to stop her fall.

Next thing she was lying on the ground, winded and dazed, and Darla stood over her, berating the boys.

"You hurt Susannah," she bellowed, her anger flaring. "Get out." She pointed to the door. As soon as they'd pushed their way through the hanging plastic panels in the exhibit, she knelt beside Susannah and searched her face. "You have a cut," she whispered fearfully, pointing to a mark on Susannah's arm.

"I'm okay, I think. Can you help me up?"

"Yes." Darla almost lifted her to her feet. Thankfully the enclosure was empty.

Susannah felt woozy and worried. Darla insisted she leave the exhibit and sit down on a bench outside. Once Susannah was seated she took her phone and dialed.

"Darla, no," Susannah protested, but it was too late.

"You said you'd come, Davy. Where are you?" Darla was angry, her brown eyes intense. "Some boys pushed Susannah and she fell down. She has a cut."

Susannah heard David's low voice assuring her he was on his way. She'd fallen so awkwardly—was the baby okay? It wasn't moving. She laid one hand over her stomach protectively and tried to form a prayer for help.

"We're really sorry." The boys had returned to apologize. "We didn't mean to bump into you."

Susannah opened her mouth but Darla spoke first.

"You should be more careful," Darla lectured. "A butterfly exhibit isn't a good place to fool around. And you shouldn't make fun of people, either," she added, her face very severe.

"Yeah, we know," the bigger one said with a sheepish grin. "You were just doing your job. Sorry, miss."

As they left, Susannah shifted, feeling bruised and uncomfortable.

"You shouldn't have phoned him, Darla. I'll be fine. It was just a little fall."

"At your stage, there are no little falls," David said, striding up to them. He knelt, touching the mark on her arm before his fingers slid down to thread with hers. He squeezed them and closed his eyes. "Woman, you scared the daylights out of me."

To her shock he gathered her in his arms and held her close.

"I'm sorry." Susannah marveled at how right it felt to be held like this. But then she noticed how pale he was, and that his hand trembled as it smoothed back her hair. "I'm fine, David."

"We're going to make sure of that," he said grimly. "You have a bruise on your chin." His jaw clenched.

"It's nothing." She wouldn't tell him how off balance she felt.

"Shall I carry you?" David held her as if he'd never let her go.

"Of course not. I can still walk." She touched his face, smoothed away the lines on his forehead, completely overwhelmed by his concern. "I'm really all right, David," she whispered.

"I'd prefer to hear that from a doctor," he growled. "Darla, tell the lady you have to leave now."

"Okay." She hurried away but was back in a flash. "Ready."

"All right, you walk on one side of Susannah. I'll walk on the other," David directed. "We'll go slowly. Okay?"

At least he waited for her nod of approval, Susannah mused. But truthfully, she was very glad of his support.

A hint of fear that she'd messed up again would not leave her.

Please don't take my baby, she silently prayed. *Please?*

Deep in her heart Susannah repeated the words Connie had been telling her ever since she'd arrived in Tucson. *God is the God of love.*

Chapter Twelve

God? Are you listening?

David waited outside the examining room, his heart in his throat.

She's so small, so delicate. That baby is all she has. Please, please don't let—

He couldn't bear to even let the thought develop as fear like he'd known only twice before burgeoned and clutched at his heart. The only time it had loosened its hold in the past half hour was when he'd had Susannah in his arms.

Where she belonged.

In that instant David made up his mind. He was going to tell Susannah that he loved her, just as Wade and Jared had advised. More than that, he was going to ask her to marry him.

"David?" Connie rushed up, laid a hand on his arm, her face worried. "Have you heard anything?"

"Not yet—" The words died on his lips as Susannah's doctor emerged from the room they'd taken her into. "Doctor?"

"You're David?" Dr. Grace Karrang smiled at him. "Susannah said you'd be hovering out here, waiting."

So she knew he wouldn't just leave her. Good.

"How is she?" Connie asked.

"Everything seems okay. I'll keep her overnight, just to make sure. But as far as I can tell now, Susannah and her baby are fine."

"Can I see her?" he asked.

"Yes. They'll move her to a room shortly, but you can all talk to her for a while. One at a time, though."

"You go first, Davy." Darla slid her hand into Connie's. "We'll wait."

"Thanks, sis. I'll hurry," he promised.

"It's okay, Davy." She touched his cheek, her eyes clear. "I prayed. Susannah and her baby are going to be all right."

"Yes." He kissed her forehead.

Susannah looked so petite on the bed, her skin ashen against the pristine sheet. Her hair had been pushed back off her face. Her eyes were closed.

David picked up her hand and threaded his fingers in hers.

"Susannah?"

She blinked a couple of times before those incredible lashes lifted and she smiled. His Sleeping Beauty.

"Hello, David. I guess I drifted off." Her soft, sweet voice sounded like music to him. "You're pale. Are you all right?"

"Me? I'm fine. It's you I'm worried about." He couldn't stop brushing his thumb against her skin, reassuring himself that she was alive and well. "How are you?"

"A little tired. The doctor said I have to stay here overnight." She frowned. "That's going to be expensive."

"It's taken care of. Don't worry." When she licked her lips, David poured a little water from the carafe and held it to her mouth. "Sip slowly."

"Thank you." She leaned back, smoothed the cover over her stomach. "I'm sorry if I worried you."

"Of course I was worried."

"Because I let this happen." She squeezed her eyes closed. "You think I'll let something happen with Darla, too. You want me to quit." She stared at him. "Is that it?"

"No!" He frowned. "I care about what happens to you, Susannah. I care a lot."

"You do?" She stared at him in disbelief, emerald eyes wide in her pale face.

"Susannah, I'm in love with you. I have been for some time." David waited to see how she'd react.

"In love—with me." She peeked at him through her lashes, then hid her eyes.

What if she still loved the baby's father? The idea hadn't occurred to him before. He couldn't think about that now—he just needed to show her.

"I've known how I felt for a while." He loved the way she let him finish his stumbling admission. "I just wasn't sure what to do about it. Until today."

"W-what have you decided?" she whispered, worry filling her face.

"Why do you always expect the worst?" he asked with tender mirth.

"I don't. Not always," she argued, her feistiness back.

"Susannah." He smiled, cupping her face in his palms. "I want to marry you, Susannah. I want you to stay with Darla and me forever. I want a future with you."

"And the baby?" she asked, fear in the shadows of her eyes. "What about my baby?"

"You'll have to learn to share because it will be our baby. Every bit as much mine and Darla's as yours," he said firmly, holding her gaze. "We'll raise him or her together. With love and laughter and faith in God."

"My faith in God isn't very strong right now," she whispered, tears welling in her eyes.

"It'll grow. We'll both work on trusting God."

Susannah studied him without speaking. David could see she was thinking deep and hard and he could only pray that she would at least think about his proposal.

"Susannah, you're not the only one who has made mistakes," he admitted, loving the feel of her skin as he caressed her face. "I let failed relationships from the past influence me into thinking God didn't want me to love again. I knew I was beginning to care for you, but I assumed I was supposed to remain single, for Darla."

"David, I—" she started, then faltered.

"You've shown me that Darla and I both need you in our lives." He slid his arms around her, drawing her close. Then he leaned forward and touched her lips with his. To his surprise, she returned his kiss with a sweetness he'd only dared dream about.

David felt relief wash over him. Maybe, just maybe, somewhere deep inside, she had at least some feelings for him. He felt joy welling up inside him.

"I love you, Susannah. And so does Darla. She would love to have a sister."

"She was like a mother bear today, protecting her cub." She smiled reflectively and reached up to smooth his hair. "Darla is amazing. You're pretty amazing, too," Susannah whispered shyly, brushing her fingers against his cheek. "Thank you for getting me here so quickly."

"I love you. How could I do anything else?" he asked, content to savor the pure bliss of holding her in his arms. "Anyway, I was scared stupid. You were so pale. Still are."

David waited but Susannah didn't respond with the words he wanted to hear. He told himself to be patient. She needed time, he reasoned. He'd sprung it on her. He kissed her quickly, then rose.

"Darla's champing at the bit to get in here. And Connie. I'll give them a turn."

"Okay." She let him go, her arms dropping to the bed.

"Susannah?"

"Yes?"

"Will you think about my proposal?" he asked, his heart jammed into his throat.

"I have to think it over. Marriage isn't something to be rushed into." Her green eyes held shadows. "I did that before and I made some huge mistakes. I'm not going to make them again."

She hadn't said yes.

But neither had she said no.

"Take all the time you need," he said as a giant geyser of hope flowed inside his heart. "I'll be waiting."

"Thank you." He turned to leave but she stopped him by catching his hand. "David?"

"Yes?"

"Will you do me a favor?" Her eyes grew huge in her small face.

He wanted to say yes, but he had a hunch he wasn't going to like it. So he quirked an eyebrow upward and waited.

"Can we not tell the others?" Her eyes were turbulent like the sea during a tempestuous storm. "Not yet anyway."

The geyser of hope inside sputtered. "Because?"

"Because I need this to be between us for now," she

whispered. "There's another life at stake. I have to make the right decision."

He wasted several moments studying her then nodded, squeezed her hand and left. "Your turn," he said to an eager Darla.

Wade stood in the hallway.

"Connie went to get some coffee," he explained. "So?"

"I asked her to marry me. She wants to think about it." David studied his friend. "She also wants to keep my proposal quiet. For now."

"So we'll pray. Hard."

"Thanks." David had laid his heart out there. What more could he do but trust that God would see him through?

While he walked on tenterhooks.

David loved her?

Susannah couldn't quite assimilate that knowledge and there wasn't time anyway. Darla burst through the doorway and came bounding over to the bed.

"Is the baby all right?" she whispered. "Are you?"

"We're both just fine. Thanks to you." Susannah hugged her. "I don't know what I would have done without you there, Darla."

"But I wasn't good," Darla countered, her face glum. "I got mad and yelled at those guys."

"You know, sometimes anger is a good thing," Susannah told her, patting the side of her bed so Darla would sit near. "Sometimes we have to get angry against injustice or when somebody does something wrong so that the wrong gets corrected. You did very well and I'm proud of you."

"Really?" Darla's huge smile lit up the room.

"Really. Thank you for protecting me. It's just the kind of thing one sister would do for another," she said quietly. "That's how I think of you, you know. As my little sister."

"I love you, Susannah." Darla hugged her enthusiastically. "And I love the baby, too." She patted her rounded stomach. "Hello, Baby."

Susannah listened to her talking to the child in her body and marveled at the love she felt for this wonderful girl. How was it possible to feel such a bond with Darla? What strange coincidence was it that Darla had slipped into her heart and nestled right next to her unborn child?

She said as much to Connie after Darla left. Her old friend simply smiled.

"It's not coincidence, Susannah," Connie assured her. "It's God."

Susannah wasn't sure about that. God didn't seem quite so personal to her, though she'd been trying to breach the gap between them by reading the Bible Connie had left in her room and taking time each night to pray.

"See, that's the thing about God," Connie said. "His love doesn't hiccup when we make mistakes or turn away from him. His love isn't like human love, Susannah. And He never, ever turns us away."

Rick Green had said the same thing, Susannah remembered.

"God's love never changes, no matter what." Connie shook her head. "There's a verse in the Bible that says nothing can separate us from the love of God. The verse goes on to list a whole bunch of things and then repeats that none of them, nothing can come between us and the love God has for His precious children."

"I hear that" she admitted, "but then it sounds like there's a *but*."

"The *but* is us, Suze." Connie shook her head. "We forget how great the love of God is, or we think we're too bad, or that we've done something too terrible." A serious note lowered her voice. "But the Bible says nothing can stop God's love."

It sounded nice, Susannah thought. Comforting, if only she could believe it. But Connie had no idea about her past, about the things she'd done since she'd left the foster home. And Susannah had no intention of telling her.

"We need to move Ms. Wells to a room now. You can see her later."

Susannah was glad for the nurse's intrusion. She wished her friend goodbye.

As they moved her to her room, she couldn't shut out that inner voice that kept offering hope. Connie's words made her wish for the impossible. But in her heart of hearts Susannah couldn't quite believe that God's love extended to her.

David claimed to love her, too. His words pinged into her brain. Was it real love he felt? How could he love someone like her?

You're pregnant with another man's child. You are so dependent on Connie and Wade you don't even have your own place. What is there to love?

But David *had* said he loved her.

And she loved him. Why deny it any longer? He'd snuck into her heart, a bit each day. She'd simply refused to let herself believe that such love could ever be returned.

For a moment, Susannah let herself bask in the knowledge of what David's love could mean. Happiness. Peace

at last. Contentment. A home for her and her baby, a
husband who cared about her, loved her and would help
her make the right decisions for the future. A sister to
share with—something Susannah had missed for so long.
She wouldn't have to be alone.

But what if she failed him? What if she did something stupid, something that embarrassed him? What
if he became ashamed of her? The thought made her
physically sick. She admired David so much, but could
she live up to what he'd expect? Did she dare risk loving
again?

The pros and cons circled her brain as Susannah
struggled to envision exactly how her life would change
if she said yes to David. The images were dazzling, allur-
ing and so far beyond anything Susannah knew that she
could hardly believe in a life like that. He would come
this evening, however. And by then she had to have her
answer ready.

Connie had said God loved her. Susannah wasn't sure
that was possible. But surely He could help her.

God? Don't let me make another mistake. Please?

Susannah curled up in the armchair behind the curtain
and inhaled the heady fragrance from the lush bouquet
of crimson roses David had sent. Her fingers trailed over
the words on the enclosed note. *For Susannah. With
love, David.*

To be loved just for yourself—how wonderful that
would be. As she fingered the velvet petals, for a moment
she let herself dream that she could actually live the
happily ever after of Darla's beloved fairy tales.

Dare she dream?

"What does that hunky lawyer see in our white-trash
girl?"

Susannah froze at the voices coming from the other bed in her room. She huddled tighter into the curtain and prayed they wouldn't see her.

"Watch it." A nurse's aide checked Susannah's bed. "She's not there. Be careful what you say, will you? She might overhear us."

"She's having a shower. Primping, no doubt," the other nurse's scathing voice condemned. "A man like him, from a wealthy family—he could have his pick of women. Why send *her* roses? She's nothing. Nobody. What's she got to offer him—an illegitimate kid?"

They left moments later but the damage was done. Even Susannah's gorgeous roses couldn't erase those harsh words from her brain. Over and over they replayed, driving the shaft of pain deeper into her heart.

Why did they have to ruin it?

Because they were right. Susannah Wells wasn't worthy of David Foster's love.

The harsh truth smacked her with reality. It was an illusion, a fantasy to think she could marry him. And she couldn't afford to deal in daydreams when her baby's future depended on her making rational, sensible choices.

Susannah shook off the fairy tale, rose from her dream world and prepared for her meeting with David. Her heart cried out to God, begging Him to help her say the hardest thing she'd ever had to say.

"You're a wonderful man, David." Susannah's voice was quiet yet he heard every word. "You're gentle, caring, kind. You'd make a wonderful husband."

"But not for you." He sat down, amazed by the decimation that rushed to swamp him. Was it possible for love to root so deeply in such a short time? *Yes,* his heart thumped. "Is it because you think I won't love your baby?"

"No."

He felt relief that she knew him that well, at least.

Susannah shook her golden head, her green eyes darkening. "That's the last thing I'd worry about. You would be the best father any child could have."

"You don't love me?" He noted the way her glance veered from his.

"I'm sorry, David. I can't accept your proposal."

"Why?" he demanded, ashamed of his desperate need to know.

"I can't use you like that," she whispered, her face sad.

"Use me?" He didn't get it.

"David, I'd ruin your life—embarrass you and Darla. Eventually you'd be ashamed when you realized I'm not someone worthy of being your wife." She put her hand over her mouth and looked down.

"Ashamed of you?" he scoffed. "That's ridiculous. I've always been very proud of you."

"Thank you for saying that." Susannah hesitated, then shook her head. "But I can't marry you, David. I'm sorry. I think the best thing is for me to give my baby a chance with someone who won't mess up as I have, someone who will make sure he or she grows up happy. That way I won't risk making another mistake."

"Won't you?" He studied her. "Or will you be making the biggest mistake of all?"

She met his gaze but said nothing.

So that was it? He'd gambled, taken a chance on telling her his true feelings, and lost. Now he was supposed to just give up?

"You haven't said anything about love, Susannah."

"I—uh—"

David tilted her chin so she had to look at him. "Do you love me?"

She didn't speak but her green eyes flashed a warning not to push.

"So you won't risk even saying the words, let alone allow yourself to feel love." He shook his head. "How sad that is—because I know you care for me. I think you love me almost as much as I love you."

"David—"

"Don't you see, Susannah? Your fear has taken over." He had to make her understand. "It controls you so much you won't let yourself believe that you can be more than the past. You won't stretch your mind and imagine yourself living with love, being the mother your child needs, being the wife I believe you can be."

"Don't waste your feelings on me—"

"Waste?" he scoffed. "It's not a waste for me to love you, Susannah. It's a joy and a privilege. You enrich my life, you make it worth living. I finish work as fast as I can so I can come home and see you, talk to you and listen to your laugh."

She looked at him, eyes welling with tears. "I'm not worth loving."

"Then you don't know Susannah as I do because I find you eminently lovable," he insisted. "I can hardly wait to hear how you're feeling and learn what you did each day. I ache to be included in your life, to be part of it all, to help you plan for that child."

She was shaking her head but David couldn't stop. He was desperate to make her understand the place she'd carved out for herself in his heart.

"Do you want to know how much I care about you, Susannah?" He should have felt embarrassed to be so needy, but he didn't. He was fighting for his future and that demanded honesty. "I question Darla every night to make sure nothing's wrong, that you didn't get too tired, that you weren't bored. I make her repeat conversations just so I can be part of your world. I can't get enough of you."

"David—"

"I love you and your child, Susannah. So don't pretend it's to spare my feelings that you're turning me down."

"I am trying to spare you," she insisted. "My past isn't—"

"You're past is not you," he said fiercely. "Not who you are today, or who you could be tomorrow. You are not that little Susannah your mother blamed."

"Yes, I am."

"No. What you are is an amazing woman who doesn't spare herself for others. You've made an endless number of good choices since you came here. But all you can do is look backward and focus on the past." Frustration surged inside him. "Why won't you risk being more than the old Susannah? Why aren't you willing to stretch yourself to be the mother your child needs?"

"People don't change, David," she whispered. "Not that much."

"You have."

"I fell for a man who lied to me, and I believed his lies." She sniffed, head bent, refusing to look at him.

His heart ached for her but he resolved to keep fighting.

"Okay, so you fell for the wrong man. Did you ever ask yourself why?" David grabbed her hands and hung on. "Because you didn't trust your inner warnings. That was a mistake people make every day."

"A bad one." Despair edged her voice.

"So?" He had to help her understand what she was throwing away. "You aren't that person anymore. You've grown, matured and taken responsibility for a baby. You've changed my life and certainly Darla's. You have a lot to give, Susannah. And by refusing to accept love, you're cheating all of us."

"I'm not cheating anyone." She yanked her hands from his. Bright spots of pink dotted her cheeks as she glared at him. "Don't you dare say that!"

Good, he wanted her to get worked up about her future and stop passively accepting what her mother had told her.

"You're cheating all of us, including yourself. But mostly you're cheating God." David hunkered down to see into her eyes. "He's given you a chance to change the course of your life, Susannah. He's given me a deep, strong love for you that can withstand your past. And I believe you share that love. Are you going to accept His gift, or throw it away?"

He held his breath, waiting, praying, hoping.

An announcement came on asking visitors to leave the hospital. David ignored it. A nurse ducked her head in and told him visiting hours were over. He ignored that, too. And waited.

Finally Susannah inhaled. Then she straightened, met his gaze directly and shook her head.

"I'm sorry, David. Thank you for your proposal, but I have to refuse." No quaver in her voice, no hesitancy—nothing that exposed what she was feeling inside. "You don't know how I wish that I could be the person you think I am. But I'm not."

"That's it? You're just going to walk away from everything—me, your child, Darla, your future? God?"

"No, I'm planning my future the best way I know how." Her voice was firm. "And I've made a decision."

David knew he wasn't going to like the next part.

"I'm resigning, David." Her big green eyes emptied of all emotion. "I promised Darla I'd take her to the pre-Easter presentation at the desert museum. That's in two weeks. It should be enough time for you to find someone else to work with Darla."

"And the baby?" he managed to choke out.

"I want to thank you for all your help, David, but I think it's better if I find someone to adopt my child on my own," she murmured. "But I will pay you what I owe you."

"Money? Will that make you feel better, Susannah?" he asked as bitterness welled.

"Yes." She lifted her chin. "Being able to pay what I owe is something I haven't always been able to do. That's just one of the things you don't know about me."

David couldn't think of a response that wouldn't dump all his anger and hurt and frustration on her, and Susannah, with her pale cheeks and hurting eyes, didn't need the extra grief.

So he did the only thing he could.

He leaned forward and kissed her, pouring all the love he felt into that kiss. To his joy, she responded. When he finally drew back, they were both breathless.

"I love you, Susannah. That isn't going to change, no matter what you do or where you go. And because I love you, I will support whatever decision you make." He smiled, touched her cheek. "You see, I have no worry about you. I know your heart. Maybe better than you do."

He walked out of the room without looking back.

But his soul wept for all he'd lost.

Chapter Thirteen

Tucson's warm desert wind stole moisture the way it stole energy. Susannah was drained.

She'd expected her last two weeks with Darla to be problematic, and they were. But not for the reasons she expected.

For one thing, Darla kept asking her about the baby and Susannah had no definitive answer.

Then there was David. He didn't press her to change her mind about marriage, didn't ask her why and didn't insist she rethink her decision. In fact, Susannah scarcely saw him, though each day there was some small reminder that he'd said he loved her.

A jar of the gourmet pickles she loved, a little book about the hilarious woes of pregnancy, a pretty bouquet in pinks or blues or both, a box of luscious chocolates, trinkets that were original and thoughtfully chosen, never duplicated.

Each one would appear with Susannah's name carefully printed on the tag in his precise writing with "Love, David" etched beneath. His manners were faultless when he arrived at home in the evening, and his demeanor as considerate as anyone could ask for. He was everything a good friend would be—kind, considerate and very gentle.

Except Susannah wanted more.

Which was totally unreasonable, and she knew it. She'd refused his proposal. She couldn't expect him to hold her when she felt ugly and horrible, or understand that she ached to hear a word of encouragement. She waited, but he never inquired about her most recent doctor's visit or commented on the fact that her feet had become all but invisible.

But she wanted that. She wanted all of it. Badly.

Each day when she left his house in the evening, he said the same thing.

"I love you, Susannah." Then he kissed her.

And each night she sat awake with her child doing acrobatics inside her, and wished the fairy tale she dreamed about could come true.

Susannah's days were full as she escorted Darla to her programs, watching the girl blossom with confidence in every activity. One evening she sat Darla down and told her she would be leaving shortly. Darla didn't argue, as she'd expected. Instead she accepted Susannah's words, hugged her tightly and told her she loved her. Then she'd disappeared to her room. Later Susannah heard her weeping.

Susannah found herself in tears often. It was so hard to think of never watching her child grow, take her first step, stumble and know she wouldn't be there to see that baby walk. Her heart squeezed tight whenever she realized she would never hear her child say "Mommy." She felt a special bond with her baby now, a secret flush of wonder each time a tiny leg stretched or a hand reached up. The wonder of this life had turned her prayers to

God into pleas for help to do the hardest thing she'd ever contemplated.

But God didn't seem to be listening, because the ache intensified right along with her feelings of worthlessness. That, more than anything, reinforced her belief that she couldn't be a mom.

The warm spring air added a precious clarity to Susannah's days as the desert began to bloom and come alive in ways she'd never imagined. One afternoon Connie drove her out to the desert museum so she could get her bearings for her trip with Darla the following week, and to witness the first burst of cactus flowers.

"I never imagined there were so many cacti," Susannah said when they'd wandered the paths for a while.

"Those are hedgehog, those are fishhook and those are saguaro cacti," Connie pointed out. "Don't walk there," she warned, grabbing Susannah's arm and drawing her back. "That's a Jumping Cholla and its spines are nasty."

So many dangerous things in this world. Would her child's adoptive mother be sure to protect her baby from all of them?

"This will all be decorated for Easter. It's unbelievable. We came last year and Silver was tongue-tied for at least ten minutes." Connie chuckled and waved a hand. "There will be specially trained museum volunteers all over the place. They'll be wearing white shirts. They can answer questions about the plants and animals in the Sonoran Desert—pretty well any that Darla can think up, I'm sure."

"She wants to know everything." Susannah smiled as pride swelled inside. "I think she wants to be a docent. Someday."

"It would be perfect for her." Connie took her arm to

steer her away from the cactus garden. "You look tired, Suze. There's a café. Let's stop and relax. We can get some coffee. Or tea."

"And maybe some sorbet?"

"Sure." Connie giggled. "You and Darla seem to share a fondness for that treat."

"Yeah. Only she prefers pistachio and I love key lime." Susannah laughed and pretended everything was fine, but inside she wept. She and Darla had grown so close. Who would love and care for this sister of her heart?

David. At least she knew Darla would be safe with him.

It was a relief to sit in the shade of the cottonwood trees and sip their hot drinks in between spoonfuls of frosty sorbet. Nearby a rock-surrounded garden burgeoned with the buzz of bees from the pollination gardens and cut the stillness of the warm afternoon.

"How are you feeling?" Connie asked.

"Big. Ugly. Tired." Susannah forced a smile. "I don't seem to be able to sleep much at night anymore." She touched her stomach. "She's always dancing."

"Or maybe *he's* playing football," Connie teased. "Are you sure you'll be well enough to trail around here with Darla? You're getting awfully close to your due date, aren't you?"

"Not that close. The doctor says I probably have at least two more weeks, and I will most likely go overdue." Susannah made a face. "How much bigger can I get?"

"You're so small, it just shows a lot. You look beautiful," Connie reassured. She was silent for several minutes before asking, "How are things with David?"

Tired of being alone and struggling to sort out her confusing feelings, Susannah had confided in Connie after David's hospital visit. Connie hadn't been surprised to hear of David's proposal. Susannah had a hunch her friend had long since guessed at her feelings, too.

"He's fine, I guess. Very busy at work, I think, but he always takes time to compliment me about something each evening." She didn't tell her friend about the good-night I love you's that kept her awake. "He keeps leaving me little gifts." Susannah tipped back her head and let the breeze cool her neck. "I feel guilty but he won't stop no matter what I say."

"Don't you like his gifts?" Connie asked, frowning.

"Oh, yes. I like being surprised by them." Susannah called herself a fool to be so transparent. "Yesterday he left the catalogue from the college. He's gathered a lot of information on the courses I will need to take to get my degree. I didn't think he'd even heard me talk about it."

"Good thing you'll have the summer to get used to the baby's schedule." Connie smiled. "You can start your program in the fall and then add as you feel able."

"I probably should have told you this before," Susannah murmured, knowing it was way past time to tell her friend. "But I'm going to give the baby up for adoption."

"Oh, Suze." Connie's eyes brimmed with tears.

"I can't keep this baby," she said firmly. "I'm a horrible role model."

"That's not true." Connie reached out and squeezed her hands, her face serious. "Listen, Susannah, I know you've been working hard to rebuild a relationship with God. Well, part of that needs to include letting the past go. It says in the Bible that God remembers our sins no more. If He can forget, why can't you?"

"David said the same thing. I haven't thought much about it," she said.

"Well, think about it now," Connie insisted.

"Why?" Susannah asked. "What difference will it make?"

"It will help you understand why you shouldn't keep hanging on to guilt from the past," Connie said, her voice stern. "When God forgives, it's gone. He doesn't keep going back and harping on it over and over. What good does His forgiveness do if we keep bashing ourselves over the heads with our mistakes?"

"But you don't know—" Susannah gulped.

"No, I don't. But the thing is, God knows, Suze. And He's forgiven it all."

Susannah sipped her tea and wondered how it felt to be clean, forgiven, made all right.

"Suze, there's always been part of your story that you held back. All that time at the farm—I've always known you never told me everything that happened with that fire." Connie squeezed her fingers.

A shadow fell over them. They glanced up. David stood staring at Susannah. It was clear he'd overheard Connie's last remarks.

"David?" Connie blinked.

"Wade sent me. Silver fell off her bike. He wants you to meet them at the hospital." He shook his head when she rushed to her feet. "She's fine, just needs a stitch. Darla's with her but she's calling for you."

"I'll go with you." Susannah pushed away her glass.

"No, stay. David can bring you back." Connie glanced at him, waiting for his nod.

"Yes, I can. No problem. In fact, I could use a drink myself. It's hot this afternoon. Drive carefully," he said to Connie.

"I will. See you later, Suze?" It was a question.

Susannah knew Connie was asking if she'd be all right with David. "Go, Connie. And kiss Silver for me."

David hailed a passing vendor and purchased a drink. Then he sat down across from her, his stare intense.

"What?" she said, feeling as if she was under a microscope.

"I overheard Connie. And I agree with her. I think you have held back something that happened at that fire." He leaned forward, touched her cheek with a forefinger. "I think you need to say it, to get it out so you can forget it."

"I'll never forget," Susannah said bleakly.

"Why?"

"Because I was the cause of that fire." She couldn't look at David, couldn't bear to see the condemnation in his eyes. "I am the reason my sisters died."

"I don't believe it." He shook her head, as if that put an end to it.

"Believe it. I left a pan on the stove. It used to get so dry in our house in Illinois in the winter. I got nosebleeds sometimes. My mother told me that if I kept a pan of water on the stove, the moisture would help. So that's what I did." She gulped as the memories flooded back, then turned to look at David. "I didn't turn it off before I left. It must have burned dry, got too hot and caught on a dishtowel or something. I was mad, you see. I wanted to get away and I never checked…"

The tears would not be stopped, grief for years of trying to erase the images of her little sisters alone, crying for help.

"Oh, Susannah." David shifted his chair nearer and wrapped a loving arm around her shoulder. "Sweetheart, you were too young to be responsible for any of that— even if it did happen that way, and I'm not sure it did."

"It did." She scrubbed her cheeks, irritated by her emotions. Good thing she had said no to David. This was just something else he'd be ashamed of.

"It doesn't matter what happened. Don't you understand? God doesn't say that one mistake is worse than another, that He'll forgive some things but not all." David smoothed her hair, his voice brimming with love that soothed. "He says 'I forgive' and He means everything. Whatever it is. And He wants you to forgive yourself, too. He wants you to enjoy a full life, to experience love and joy. He planned that especially for you, Susannah."

"I've done a lot of things I'm ashamed of."

David only smiled.

"Doesn't matter," he said. "You asked for forgiveness and God gave it. He doesn't hold it against you. He knows you, Susannah. He knows you were young and mixed up and hanging with the wrong group. He knows who you are, everything that you've done, and He loves you anyway."

"I don't understand how that could be." Susannah listened as David explained more about forgiveness on the way home. And she promised him she'd try and forgive herself for her past.

But late that night, as she sat on the window seat watching the moon slide in and out behind clouds, Susannah knew that while forgiveness might be possible, forgetting was not. She would carry those scars of guilt for the rest of her life.

And she couldn't bear it if her child found out. Adoption was the only way.

"So you're saying Susannah Wells's mother is still in jail?" David scribbled the information on a pad to study later.

"Not still—again. And not exactly jail," the social worker said. "It's a facility to help Mrs. Wells deal with her personal issues. But yes, she has been committed to staying there until the doctors feel she can handle life on the outside. Given her refusal to accept any responsibility for her recent actions, my understanding is that she will not be leaving soon." The social worker listed the most recent charges that had been added to Mrs. Wells's latest sentence.

She wouldn't give him specific details, of course. And David hadn't expected any.

"The lady has a problem with responsibility," she finished.

"Me, too," David muttered after he'd hung up.

But his problem was of another kind. He'd been so preoccupied with being overwhelmed with responsibility, he now realized he'd missed out on a lot of what life offered. Now he desperately craved the opportunity to be responsible for Susannah and the life she carried. But she would have none of it.

And he didn't know what to do about that.

For years after his father's death, David had believed he had to be in control of everything in his world. But when Susannah came along, she'd inadvertently forced him to realize that he needed to surrender the controls of his life. Recently Wade and Jared, too, had helped him realize he needed to completely surrender his past, present and future to God.

"Jared Hornby is on line two." His secretary cut into his thoughts.

David picked up the phone.

"You called?"

"Yeah." David proposed lunch with his old friend. "I need to pick your brain again," he explained.

"Oh, so then you'd be buying," Jared said. "Great. I'm not far away. Fifteen minutes at Scarfies? We haven't been there in ages."

"Okay." David left the office immediately. He needed to get outside, breathe the fresh spring air and think as he walked the few blocks to their favorite lunch place. But when he arrived, his brain was more knotted than ever.

Jared sat waiting, his iced tea half gone.

"Hi." David hurriedly ordered the special. When Jared had placed his order and their server had left, he cleared his throat. "I feel like I'm drowning," he said.

"Susannah," Jared guessed.

"I believe she is God's choice for me, Jared. She's the only woman I want in my life."

"And her past?" His old friend hunched forward to study him.

David crossed his arms over his chest. "I couldn't care less about her past, except that whatever happened, it made her into the woman I love."

"You can't write it off that easily, pal." Jared shook his head. "Susannah has had some bad things happen to her. It's got to impact her."

"Where are you going with this?" David frowned.

"Wade and I advised you to tell Susannah how you felt." Jared shrugged. "Okay, you did that. And she didn't respond the way you wanted. I think you have to accept her response, buddy. I think that you have to leave the future with God." Jared sipped his iced tea.

"Just give up. That's what you mean?" Even the idea left a bad taste in David's mouth.

"Give it up to God," Jared corrected. "If she's His choice for you, let God work it out."

David shook his head. "I don't think God expects me

to sit back and do nothing here, Jared. I can't do that. What if she gives her child away?"

"David, she *is* going to give her baby away," Jared said.

"Her past and her mistakes are exactly why she has to keep that baby," he insisted. "If she doesn't, that will only be one more thing Susannah will regret."

Jared thought about it a moment. "You said her mother's blame is at the root of all her feelings of unworthiness?"

"I'm no psychologist," David said, "but I think her mother's accusation that Susannah caused her sisters' deaths left a pretty big wound, yeah."

"Maybe you should go see her mother, try and get her to show some compassion for the only daughter she has left?" Jared quirked one eyebrow.

"It's worth a try, I suppose." David hated the thought of it. Intruding into someone else's past, reopening old wounds—everything in him protested at the depth of involvement. Susannah would be furious. But if it would help her...

"I'll pray. So will Wade." Jared leaned back as their food was delivered. "We'll keep a steady line going to heaven while you talk to this woman. There's just one thing."

"Yeah?" Personally David thought there was a lot more than *one* thing, but he waited for his friend to finish.

"What if none of it makes any difference to Susannah?" he asked.

David stalled, taking a bite of his burger and chewing it thoroughly. Finally he met Jared's gaze.

"I don't know," he admitted. "I can't think that far ahead."

* * *

"I don't know you." The woman flopped herself into the easy chair, her silver-blond hair tumbling to her shoulders. A more mature Susannah. "Do I?"

"No. David Foster. I'm a friend of Susannah's."

A spark of interest lit the green eyes before she covered with a lackluster shrug. He held out a hand, which she declined to shake.

"Your daughter Susannah," he said as anger surged up.

"I haven't seen her in years." Sara Wells looked at him balefully.

"Since the fire." He nodded. "I know. Why is that?"

"Look," she bristled, "I don't know who you think you are or why you're poking your nose into something that isn't any of your business, but—"

"It is my business." David leaned back and chose another tack. "Do you know you're going to be a grandmother?"

She leaned forward, intrigued in spite of herself.

"Congratulations." Her lips curled.

"It's not my child. But I would like it to be," he said. He felt a rush of love as the words resounded to his soul. "I love Susannah. I want to marry her. She's a wonderful woman—loving, caring, gentle and courageous."

"Everything I'm not, is that what you mean?" Her eyes darkened.

"This isn't about you," David assured her. "You cut your own daughter out of your life."

"I have my reasons."

"I know all about your reasons. To make yourself look innocent. To ease your own pain. You blamed Susannah for her sisters' deaths. That was a lie, wasn't it?"

Sara Wells remained silent.

"She was a child, a little girl with far too much responsibility."

"Do you think I don't know that?" Sara's face tightened.

"Then why?" he asked quietly. "You weren't the only one who lost. She lost her sisters. And she's spent all these years believing the lie you told her."

Tears flowed down her cheeks unchecked, but she stayed silent.

"Everything Susannah does is colored by her guilt, her belief that she was responsible," he said, but he moderated his voice because her tears touched his heart. This woman had lost her children. There was enough pain to go around.

Sara still said nothing. David knew he had to jar her out of her silence.

"This is a picture of her." He slid his favorite photo of Susannah across the table. She was daydreaming about something, staring into the lens, a small smile lifting her lips. "She's beautiful inside and out. She'd be a wonderful mother."

One hand reached out to trace the features on Susannah's lovely face. The tears did not stop. A flicker of empathy rose inside David's heart for this woman—she'd never known the wonderful beauty of what her child had become in spite of her.

"She's going to give away her baby to someone else, to adopt, because she thinks she's unworthy and because she's afraid she won't be the kind of mother she wants to be," David explained.

"She thinks she'll be like me. A drunk?" Finally Sara looked at him. Her excruciating pain engulfed him like a tidal wave and sucked all his anger away.

"She needs your forgiveness," David told her. "She

needs to hear you say that her sisters' deaths were not her fault. This pain, this hurt—hasn't it gone on long enough, Sara? Your daughter needs you. Susannah needs the mother who abandoned her all those years ago."

"I'm sorry but your time is up." A guard waited at his elbow.

David rose, but he left the picture on the table.

"Susannah's baby is due very soon," he said, keeping his voice soft. "If you're going to help her, it must be quickly, before the baby's born. Otherwise it will be too late to repair the past."

Sara simply sat there, staring at her daughter. He laid a hand on her shoulder.

"I'll pray for you, Sara. I'll ask God to heal your heart and soul and show you that He has plans for your future, something beautiful that you can't even imagine."

As he drove home, he prayed harder than he had in his entire life.

For all of them.

Susannah was miserable.

"I'm tired all the time," she told her doctor. "I can't see my toes anymore, let alone polish them. I feel like a limp rag even first thing in the morning."

"It's spring and this is the desert. It's only going to get warmer. Rest," the doctor advised.

"That's what everyone says," Susannah complained. "I do almost nothing but rest, and I'm still tired."

"Then rest some more. You're carrying a baby, Susannah. That's hard work. Probably the hardest job you'll ever have. You have to save your strength. Did you go to those Lamaze classes?"

"Yes." She'd gone with Connie and Darla. Precious,

poignant, bittersweet evenings, full of laughter and tears.

"So you're ready," the doctor said. "Now you're just going to have to wait patiently until this baby decides its arrival date. Relax."

Connie also kept telling her to slow down but Susannah was frantic to find a family for her baby, and without David's help she floundered. How could you know about anyone's real intent through an internet profile?

As she made her way to pick up Darla, Susannah realized anew how difficult she was finding it, keeping up with Darla's activities, though her charge was always solicitous about Susannah's health. Darla fussed about the baby constantly, monitoring what Susannah ate and when. She insisted Susannah take frequent rests and offered water so often Susannah worried she'd float away during soccer practice or while waiting for Darla at the botanical garden. She made her way into David's house with Darla dancing attendance.

"Sixty-seven percent of pregnant women do not drink enough water," Darla declared. She was quoting statistics less often now, but the odd one still popped out whenever she wanted to defend her actions.

"I'm fine, Darla. Oh." The Braxton-Hicks contraction grabbed and held on, forcing Susannah to sit down on David's sofa and wait it out. "We'll make cookies in a little while," she promised with a gasp.

"Okay." Darla flopped down at the coffee table. "I'm going to draw some of the butterflies from the botanical garden so I can show the people at the center what I do." She plugged in her headphones and began humming to the music as her fingers flew across the page.

Once the tension in her stomach relaxed, Susannah closed her eyes. Just for a minute. Then she'd get up and make the cookies Darla wanted to take to school tomorrow. As she lay there, the scent from roses David had cut from the garden filled her senses. How wonderful to have your own rose bushes.

It was just one of the things Susannah was going to miss about this job. Each day had proven harder than the one before as she realized exactly what she was giving up by refusing David's proposal. Once she took Darla to the desert museum, her lovely life here would be over and all she'd have left were memories.

"I'm only asking You for one thing, God," she whispered. "Just please make sure my baby is healthy."

The house was quiet when he arrived home. Too quiet.

David tucked the packet of key lime-flavored mints under Susannah's purse. She'd mentioned she liked them last week, so today, on the way home, he'd made a special trip to the candy store to get them for her.

Not that she'd said it specifically to him. She hadn't. Susannah barely said two words to him anymore, and if she did, she made sure to keep her gaze averted. Ever since he'd proposed she'd been shy around him—hesitant, quiet.

But that didn't stop David from noting her likes and dislikes—Susannah liked lime-flavored anything, and it gave him great pleasure to seek out little gifts and leave them for her enjoyment. He'd wait like a kid and watch for her to discover his surprise, and then treasure that moment when she closed her eyes and hugged the treat to her heart.

Those few seconds made the bereft moments in his life bearable. That and the way she leaned into his nightly embrace before she remembered and pulled away....

David was going to call out, but then he stepped into the family room and saw Darla flopped on the floor, her headphones in her ears, her eyes closed. Her chest moved up and down in a soft, rhythmic snore. He found Susannah lying on the sofa with her eyes closed and a faint smile on her lips as she dozed.

Darla's Sleeping Beauty.

One hand lay on top of her stomach, as if to protect the precious life within. Mother and child. Was there anything more beautiful?

He wondered again about Susannah's mother. Would she do the right thing? Or would she stay in her self-imposed prison? Once more he prayed for the troubled Sara and asked God to release her heart so that she could reach out to the daughter who needed peace so badly.

David spent some time just watching Susannah, treasuring the moment because he didn't know when it might happen again. One more day, that's all she had left to work for him. Then—who knew?

"Oh, I didn't realize it was so late." She blinked at him, then struggled to sit up, grasping David's hand when he held it out, easing herself off the sofa. "Thank you. I feel like an elephant."

"You look beautiful," he murmured. He touched her cheek with his fingers and pressed a kiss against her forehead. "Very beautiful."

She gave him a look that said she thought he was fibbing.

"I mean it. Your skin has this amazing luminosity— it's very attractive," he said, finishing hurriedly, amazed at his newfound ability to be so poetic.

"Well." Susannah stepped around him. "I shouldn't be sleepng. Darla needs to take some cookies to school tomorrow and we haven't baked them yet."

"Let's have dinner, and then we'll make them together. I think Mrs. Peters left everything in the slow cooker."

"I don't need to stay for dinner," Susannah said. "I can come back later."

"Susannah, please. Just stay for dinner. It's not a big deal, okay?" He woke Darla, then followed them both into the kitchen.

Darla made short work of setting the table. She put the kettle on to boil for tea, lifted a salad from the fridge and a freshly made loaf of bread from the cupboard. "Everything's ready, Davy."

They sat, and as he held out his hand for Darla's to say grace, David also reached out for Susannah's.

Please let her stay permanently, he prayed silently. *She's a part of our family.*

Susannah bowed her head for the grace. The moment it was over she took her hand from his. She said little during the meal. She picked at her food, eating only a small fraction of what she was served.

"Are you all right?" he asked when Darla went to answer the phone.

"Fine. Just a little uncomfortable." She smiled ruefully. "I'll get in the pool tonight and stretch everything out. That should help."

"I'm sorry it's so hard on you," he said, touching her shoulder. "I'd do it for you, if I could."

She smiled faintly, her gaze finally meeting his. "Thank you," she whispered.

While David cleared the table, Susannah helped Darla assemble the ingredients for cookies. But when he thought it might be best to leave the two alone with their baking, Darla suddenly said she had to finish her homework. David waved her off, then noticed how Susannah flagged, leaning against the counter.

"Sit down," he ordered, easing her into a chair. "There's no need to bake cookies tonight. I can stop by a bakery tomorrow."

"Darla said everyone is bringing some from home. She wanted to do the same." She began pulling out ingredients.

"You are so stubborn." He rolled up his sleeves. "Okay, tell me what to do."

She would have argued but he guessed from the lines of weariness around her eyes that she was too tired. So he listened carefully and followed each step she gave until the batter was mixed.

"Darla and I will bake them later." David was inordinately pleased with his accomplishment.

"You don't know how to bake," she said with a frown.

"Three hundred fifty degrees for about eight minutes," he repeated, and then added before she could interrupt, "and watch they don't burn."

"But—"

"But now it's time for you to go home." He held up a hand so she wouldn't argue. "You need to take care of yourself, Susannah. And that baby."

"But this is my job," she protested, though it sounded weak.

"You have done an amazing job. Darla and I both know that. You've gone way beyond anything I ever expected." He drew her into the circle of his arms and pressed his lips against the top of her head. To his joy she rested against him and relaxed, letting him hold her. "I don't want you to overdo. Not now. So go home. Take the car. Please?" he asked, tilting her head back so he could look into her eyes.

"You're a very nice man, David," she whispered against his chest. "I wish…"

So did he. Unfortunately wishing didn't make your heart's desire come true. And he couldn't badger her about it now. So David kissed her tenderly, then set her away from him.

"Go home and rest," he ordered.

He waited while she gathered up her handbag. Her hand paused on the mints. She lifted her head to stare at him, green eyes shiny with tears.

"Thank you," she whispered.

"It's my pleasure." And it was. Whatever he could do for her was so little and he only wanted to do more. "I love you."

She searched his eyes, touched his cheek with her small delicate fingers then reached for the door.

"Good night," she whispered.

He watched her get in the car, pull out and drive away as his sister emerged.

"Tomorrow is Susannah's last day, Davy. Then what will we do?" Darla's hand curved into his. Her troubled eyes searched his for reassurance.

"I don't know, Darla. Keep loving her, I guess."

"And pray."

Yeah. Pray.

Lord?

But the only answer David heard was "trust."

Chapter Fourteen

"I've got to get back to the office," David said Saturday morning.

"Today? Tomorrow is Easter Sunday." Susannah had been hoping he'd volunteer to take Darla to the museum, or at least accompany them.

Truth to tell, she hadn't felt well since she'd risen. Still wasn't. She had thought about backing out of this trip, but had been unable to deny Darla when she learned David would be working. Also, Susannah had greedily wanted a few more moments together before she was permanently out of their lives.

Like so many other things, that wasn't to be.

"I wish I could go with you, but I've got a big court case next week. It's my last chance to interview some people I intend to call as witnesses." He held out an envelope. "But I wanted to personally make sure you got this."

"What is it?" She stared at the plain white envelope curiously.

"A letter. Someone asked that I give it to you." He tucked it into her purse. "Don't forget to read it, please. It might change your life."

Susannah puzzled over that and over the kiss David gave her. It was deep and rich and satisfying, but there was also a longing to it. She kissed him back in spite of herself. When he finally drew back, he kept hold of her and stared deep into her eyes.

"I love you, Susannah. I wish you could accept that, because it's not going to change." David laid a fingertip over her lips. "Don't say anything. Just know that if you ever need me, for anything, promise you'll call me. I'll come, no matter what. No matter what, Susannah."

She nodded, but she knew she would not be calling him. This was goodbye.

"The same thing is true of God," David murmured. "He's there waiting to hear from you. If you could only accept that God is about forgiveness, not condemnation. He loves you. He loves you so much He gave His only son for you. Because He thinks you are worth it." He cupped her cheek, brushed his hand over her hair and cupped the back of her neck in his palm. "All you have to do is believe it."

One last kiss, then he was gone.

"Did you see that?" Darla asked, hours later.

"Uh-huh." Susannah smiled but continued her search for a chair.

"I got that little girl to move back from the edge so she wouldn't get hurt and I didn't yell at all." Darla preened, her chest thrust out.

"I'm very proud of you." No longer appreciative of the vista in front of her, Susannah shifted from one foot to the other, trying to ease the ache in her lower back. She wanted—no needed—to sit down after tramping around the desert museum for the better part of two hours.

"I got those kids to be quiet in the underground

exhibits, too," Darla reminded. "They wouldn't listen at first, but then I explained how the animals like to sleep in the day and work at night, and the kids stopped making so much noise."

"You did a fantastic job." Susannah smoothed her hair and smiled at the triumph on Darla's pretty face. "Should we go have lunch?"

"Not yet. The docent—" Darla paused, serious. "That's what they're called, docents," she explained.

"Uh-huh." Susannah forced herself not to smile.

"Well, the docents said there is going to be a demonstration of the raptor free flights." She checked her watch. "That's in ten minutes."

Susannah wanted to groan. The raptor area was way at the back. She knew she could not walk that far right now.

"Listen sweetie, can you go with the docents and stay right beside them?" Guilt overwhelmed her at letting Darla go alone, but she'd waited so long to see the birds and the raptor flights were a seasonal thing. "I'll stay here."

"Are you sick, Susannah?" Darla tilted her head to one side and studied her with those wise-owl brown eyes. "I don't have to see the raptors," she decided.

"Yes, you do. And I'm fine. Just really tired and hot. I'm going to sit down right over there—" she pointed to the nearby coffee bar "—and wait for you. Okay?"

"Are you sure you're not sick?" Darla frowned.

"I'm not. I'm fine. I'm only tired," Susannah reassured her.

"Because of the baby," Darla said. "Pretty soon I'll see it, won't I?"

"I think so. Pretty soon." She rubbed her side as a funny little cramp uncoiled.

"I asked God to make your baby strong, Susannah. I pray for it and you every night." Darla trailed along beside her until they found a chair where Susannah could sit, still visible, but out of the hot sun.

"Thank you, sweetie. I appreciate your prayers." Susannah saw one of the many volunteers nearby. She handed Darla some money and asked her to buy two cold drinks from the vendor inside. Left alone, she waved over the docent and explained her situation.

"It's not a problem, ma'am. I'll be happy to take her to the raptors, and I'll bring her back when it's over," the girl said.

"Thank you very much." Susannah shifted, trying to find a more comfortable position.

"Are you okay? Can I get someone to help you?"

"That's very kind of you, but I just need to sit awhile. I'll be fine." When Darla returned, Susannah thanked her for the drink and introduced the girl. "You go with her and come back with her," she said firmly. "Don't wander away."

"I won't." Darla hugged her tightly. "You rest. I'll be back."

"Have fun." Susannah waited until they'd disappeared, then closed her eyes and sipped her drink. Five minutes later she felt much better.

Then she remembered the envelope in her bag.

Now Susannah lifted the envelope free and opened the flap. A single sheet of paper was inside, plain white with writing scrawled across it.

Dear Susannah:
I write that because you are dear to me. So pre-
cious. You are the best thing to come out of my
stupid, wasted life. I know that now. A daughter

*who took over when I wouldn't. How can I ever
thank you? I can't. And I owe you so much. Most
of all, I owe you an apology.*

Susannah's breath jammed in her throat as she read
on.

> *Susannah, I want you to hear me on this. And
> hear me well. You did not cause your sisters'
> deaths. I did. That night I was in a drunken stupor.
> Some ash from my cigarette fell on me and burned
> my leg and I realized the sofa was on fire, so was
> the carpet. I ran to the kitchen to get some water. I
> thought I could put it out. But it was in the drapes
> then and flaring. The smoke was so thick. I tried,
> but I couldn't reach Misty and Cara. They'd fallen
> asleep, waiting for me to tell them a story. A fire-
> man told me later that they never woke up.*

Every breath was agony as Susannah remembered
their happy, smiling faces. How could God let two
small lives be taken like that? The familiar tidal wave
of loss filled her with pain that reached into her soul and
squeezed.

Susannah wanted to stop reading. She wanted to fold
up the letter and hide it away and never look at it again.
But she couldn't. The past had dogged her for so long.
The desperate yearning to hear from her mother, long
buried deep within, now would not be silenced.

The truth.

She needed to hear the whole truth about that terrible
night.

Sniffing back her tears, she refocused on the scribbled
words.

I wanted to die with them, Susannah. I wanted to go with Misty and Cara and be rid of my awful life. But you came and found me in the kitchen and pulled me out. I hated you for keeping me alive. I wanted to die and you wouldn't let me and the pain was excruciating. So I lashed out and said it was your fault they died—because I needed to get rid of my own guilt.

Oh, Susannah, until your boyfriend came to see me, I never realized that no one had ever told you the real truth of that awful night—that you were not to blame. All these years I've kept away from you, distanced myself because the guilt and the shame were so great when I looked at you that I knew I could never be the parent you needed, that I could never be worthy of being entrusted with another child. So I pushed you away and made sure you didn't come back. But I've missed you.

David? David had gone to see her mother? But then, it fit with what she knew of him. David Foster had shown time and again that he loved her. No wonder Darla liked fairy tales. Her brother was hero stuff through and through.

Susannah, you are not like me. You never were. You are strong and courageous and the best mother to your sisters that they could have had. They loved you so much. And you loved them. It was not your fault they died. You did your best, even tried to get to them. No sister could have done more.

Susannah blinked through the tears as the devastating scene from that night replayed through her mind again. But this time it had a new part, a part she'd never recalled until now. A part where she remembered pushing open the back door, seeing her mother on the floor and dragging her outside. As if in a trance, Susannah felt the heat stinging her hands as she knocked away a burning chair and slapped at her mother's dress to put out the flames. And now she also remembered lying on the lawn, gasping for air, struggling to inhale enough oxygen to go inside and find her sisters.

She'd made it to the door before the firefighters had stopped her. They'd put a mask over her mouth and something cool on her hands. The next thing Susannah recalled was awakening in the hospital with bandages on her hands and face and a terrible sadness in her heart for the sisters she knew were gone.

For so long she'd forgotten those details. That's why her mother's screams of blame had stuck. That's why she'd never questioned that it was her fault that Cara and Misty had died. That's why she'd always felt so guilty.

Because she'd forgotten the truth. The truth.

Bemused by this new insight, she glanced down.

Your young man loves you, Susannah. Don't throw it away because of my mistakes. Love doesn't come so often that we can waste it. Your sisters would want you to be happy, to enjoy your life. I don't know much about God, but your boyfriend has made me think that He might someday forgive me.

You are more than I will ever be, Susannah. I know that no child of yours would ever be without your love. And love, more than anything, is what we need to survive. You were always fearless as a child, Susannah. Be fearless now and embrace your life.

Your mother.

She wasn't guilty. She hadn't caused their deaths. It wasn't her fault.

The words kept racing around and around her brain, rejuvenating her soul with relief and joy. After reading the precious words once more, Susannah refolded the letter and tucked it back into its envelope. A tiny slip of paper lay there. She pulled it out and read it.

It's in Christ that we find out who we are and what we are living for. Long before we first heard of Christ and got our hopes up, he had his eye on us, had designs on us for glorious living, part of the overall purpose he is working out in everything and everyone.

Ephesians 1:11-12 from The Message.

David. Dear darling David, who had gone to see her mother, dug until he found the truth and made sure Susannah knew it. David who'd said he loved her so many times and refused to give up on her. David—a man who practiced love.

Carefully, Susannah placed her precious papers in her purse. How could she ever thank him? As she sat waiting for Darla, she tried to think of ways to tell him what his actions meant to her. And yet, she couldn't do that. It would be too painful and he might think that she'd changed her mind about marrying him. Which she hadn't. Not because she didn't love him, but because she did.

Her thoughts got sideswiped by a rip of pain through her midsection. It dulled to a steady ache that would not go away even after Darla returned and they went for lunch. Susannah ate a little to keep her strength up, but as the day went on, she felt progressively worse.

"Susannah, we should go home." Darla frowned when Susannah declined to enter the aviary but insisted Darla go without her. "You're too tired."

"I just need to walk a bit more. When I walk I feel better. Go ahead. I'll be out here." But eventually even walking didn't help and when the museum announced they would be closing in five minutes, Susannah was forced to agree that they should leave. But she asked Darla to buy her some bottled water first. "I'm really thirsty," she said.

"Because it's too hot for you," Darla said. She trotted off to get the water but quickly returned, her face showing her concern. "I wish I could drive."

"I'll be fine once I'm in the air-conditioning."

Only Susannah wasn't fine. She'd no sooner sat down in the driver's seat when her water broke. She turned on the radio.

"I need a minute to hear the news," she said, desperate to keep Darla from knowing how scared she was.

The baby was coming. Susannah had read enough to know that. It was simply a matter of how long she had before it arrived. She shifted into gear and began the drive home.

She'd gone only a few miles when a fierce contraction grabbed her. Susannah pulled into a vista point along the way and told Darla to go ahead and look. As soon as Darla left the car, Susannah began breathing the way she'd learned in Lamaze class. She puffed through the contractions before Darla returned.

It was well past six now. The road from the museum was almost deserted. Easter weekend. People were home with their families. Susannah bit her lip as another contraction hit. She tried to keep her concentration on the road but they were too strong and too fast and there was so little time to regroup in between. She veered sideways and felt the car lurch to a halt as the front wheel struck a huge stone at the side of the road. The grinding sound of metal made her cringe.

"Darla, are you okay?" she asked, fighting to breathe through the ferocity of this contraction.

"Yes. I'm fine." Darla touched her hand. "Susannah, what's wrong?" She had to wait while Susannah worked her way through the pain before she could explain what was happening.

"I'm so sorry, Darla. I should never have brought you out here today." She slid her seat all the way back and caressed her fingers over her stomach, breathing more normally as the skin grew less taut. "The baby's coming."

"Now?" Darla's brown eyes widened.

"Pretty soon, I think." Again she had to stop and work her way through another contraction. They were much closer together now. And getting stronger.

"We have to pray, Susannah," Darla insisted. "We'll ask God to help us and help the baby. He loves us, Susannah. He knows about your baby and that we need help."

"Just another thing I've messed up," she muttered.

"God doesn't care about that. He always forgives, if we ask." Darla closed her eyes and began to speak to her heavenly father, asking His help. Then she opened her eyes and smiled. "God loves children," she said with supreme confidence. "In the Bible Jesus told his disciples they had to let the kids come to him. He won't let anything happen to your baby."

Susannah wished she was as sure.

"I should never have waited so long," she said, tears slipping down her cheeks as the pain began with renewed force. "How could I make such a stupid mistake?"

"I'm going to call for help." Darla took Susannah's phone and dialed 911 and in a clear, precise voice told the operator what was happening. "I can't stay on the phone," she said. "I have to call my brother, Davy."

Susannah didn't hear the rest of her conversation— she was too busy managing her breathing. When finally she was through the contraction, she heard Darla say, "Susannah is having her baby, Davy. We need help. Hurry, okay? Susannah's really scared. But I'm not. I prayed. Davy?" She frowned, shook the phone then held it out. "Something's wrong with it."

"The battery is dead," she explained after glancing at it. Terror clawed at Susannah's throat. What if something went wrong with the baby?

"Darla, I'm so sorry. I should have left earlier." Susannah searched the girl's eyes, wondering if she would panic.

"It doesn't matter, Susannah. Davy will find us." Darla used her scarf to dab some of the water from her bottle on her forehead.

"I hope somebody does. It will be dark in less than an hour. Ooh," Susannah groaned, losing a bit of her focus as the pain grew.

Darla waited until the spasm was gone.

"I don't think you can have the baby sitting there, Susannah. I think you should get into the backseat." She scooted out and around the car and in between huffing and puffing right along with Susannah, managed to get her lying in the rear seat. "Put your feet in my lap," she ordered after she'd closed and locked the doors.

Susannah got caught up in another contraction but Darla was right there with her, encouraging her to follow her breathing pattern as they'd done so often in Lamaze.

"You're doing very well, Susannah," she encouraged, smoothing back her hair as she spoke. "Don't be afraid. I remember all the steps they said you have to go through before the baby comes. I'll help you."

"I know you will, sweetie. You're a great help."

She had Darla—and God. Trusting was so hard.

After several fierce contractions, Susannah was convinced her baby's birth was imminent. She had to count on Darla's help and she had to prepare her before things progressed any further.

"Listen to me, honey."

"I'm listening." Darla remained silent and attentive as Susannah explained what she'd need.

"Do you think you can do all that?" Susannah asked.

"Yes." She nodded confidently and calmly. "I can do it. And I won't get scared, Susannah. I'll keep praying." With that simple assurance, she began assessing their resources. "There's a blanket here. Mrs. Peters put it in last week. She thought it would be good for a picnic. And we have the water. Everything is going to be okay, Susannah."

There was no other choice, Susannah realized. She had to trust that God loved her. In that moment she realized the truth of that Scripture verse David had written. God was working out a glorious purpose in her life. He'd helped her during the fire; He'd sent her to a good home to grow up in; He'd led her to David and Darla.

"Susannah?" Darla touched her hand, her wise eyes soft. "Are you okay?"

"I'm scared, Darla. What if something goes wrong? What if the baby needs help?" She wanted to trust, but she hurt so much and now the fears and worries she'd kept tamped down for so long rose in a tumult of terror. "What if I did something to hurt my baby? What if God is going to punish it because of me?"

"No, Susannah." Darla shook her head firmly. "God

isn't like that. He loves us. That's all. Love." She spread her hands.

And finally the truth penetrated to Susannah's heart. God was about forgiveness, not punishment. The guilt she felt, the condemnation she'd lived with for years—that didn't come from God. That was something she put on herself. She'd wanted her baby to be adopted because she was scared—scared to risk moving past the fear, scared to risk being hurt by loving David, scared to accept that she could be more than she'd allowed herself to dream of.

Susannah grabbed her purse and pulled out the note David had written.

It's in Christ that we find out who we are and what we are living for.

Doing things her way had resulted in nothing but trouble. Was she going to stay alone and afraid, and keep getting the same results? Or was she going to get some backbone, accept the love God offered and live her life in a newer, better way?

When she considered what was at stake, there was no contest.

"Please help me, God. Please help my baby. Please help Darla," she whispered.

A wonderful sensation of warmth suffused her, as if someone had drawn her into warm sheltering arms.

"Oh!" Susannah groaned. "Darla, I think the baby is coming. I have to push."

"That's okay," Darla said with a grin. "I'm ready. I remember everything the lady said. Seventy two per cent of births have no complications. And besides, we have God helping."

"Yes, we do," Susannah cried. And then she pushed.

Chapter Fifteen

"Oh, Lord, be with them both."

David wove in and out of traffic until he was free of the city. Then he barreled through the desert like a madman, desperate to get to Darla and Susannah. He'd wasted minutes trying to remember where they were going today, only recalling the desert museum when a frantic call to Connie had reminded him.

He still felt the shock of Darla's message. Why hadn't he answered the stupid phone, instead of letting the call go to messages? Was work so much more important than the two women in his life? Why hadn't he gone with them today?

A big lump of fear stuck in his throat as he tried again to reach their cell phone. There was still no answer. He'd contacted Susannah's doctor and received some assurance that labor in a first birth usually took its time. He could only pray that was true because he was afraid to envision anything else.

Darla had gone to the Lamaze classes. She'd regaled him with all the knowledge she'd learned. But she couldn't handle a birth. Not alone. And Susannah—this was her first child. She'd be alone, afraid and worrying she'd made another bad decision.

If only he'd—no. David wasn't going to doubt. Susannah, her baby and Darla were all in God's hands. He had Wade, Jared and Connie praying. He had to trust that God would show him how to help the woman who held his heart in her delicate hands.

Ahead David saw the flash of lights signaling an ambulance. He swerved to the side of the road before he leaped out and sprinted across. His heart almost stopped when he saw a small figure on the white stretcher.

"Susannah?"

"Davy!" Darla stood beside the ambulance. "We have a baby," she said showing him the tiny bundle tucked into Susannah's arms. "It's a girl."

"Grace," Susannah told him, her voice clear and her eyes sparkling. "Her name is Grace, David. Because of God's grace to me."

"Oh, Susannah." He bent and kissed her as his heart lifted with thanksgiving. "I love you." He gazed down at her and let the picture of mother and daughter frame in his mind. "She's beautiful, Susannah. As beautiful as you."

"We need to get them to the hospital now," one of the EMTs said.

"Yes. Go ahead." David touched her cheek with his knuckles, brushing one fingertip against the baby's velvet skin. "I'll see you at the hospital, Susannah." Then he bent and repeated, for her ears alone, "I love you."

She opened her mouth but the attendants whisked her away too quickly and he couldn't hear what she said.

"I helped get the baby, Davy! I helped." Darla danced at his side, yanking on his arm in her excitement. "Susannah said she couldn't ever have done it alone. I'm the first person Grace saw when she came in the world."

"You did really well, sis." He hugged her tightly. "I'm so proud of you."

"Me, too." She hugged him back but she couldn't stand still for more than a second. "Grace didn't cry at first. Susannah said she had to cry and she didn't so I prayed and said to God, 'God, can You make this baby cry?' And He did!"

"That's great, sweetie." He hugged her again. "You're quite a girl."

"I know."

While Darla related the events of the day, David glanced at the car Susannah had been in. He stopped Darla's story long enough to call a tow truck and his friends. Then Darla climbed into his car and they headed for the hospital.

Ecstatic over her role in the birth, Darla talked non-stop all the way. David heard little of it. He was too busy wondering how Susannah would react when the baby was adopted.

"Davy?"

"Yes?" He climbed out of his dark thoughts, noticing sadness creeping over Darla's face. "What's wrong?"

"Susannah's my sister, Davy. I don't want her or baby Grace to go away."

"Darla, honey, I explained to you about the adoption. Susannah wants another mommy to look after Grace." But Darla clamped her hands over her ears and refused to listen. She only dropped them when he stopped speaking.

"God made Susannah my sister," she said firmly. "Baby Grace is my family, too."

Nothing he could say could change her mind. But Darla didn't get angry and she didn't argue or yell.

When they got to the hospital she waited until he found Susannah's room.

"We must be very quiet when we see Susannah," he explained. "Don't ask her a lot of questions, okay?" He'd think of a way to explain it all later.

"I won't." Darla stopped a passing nurse. "Can you tell me where the babies are?" she asked.

"In the nursery." She pointed. "But only family can go down there. Are you family?"

"I'm the...aunt," Darla said proudly.

David winced. She was going to be so hurt when Grace went to another family. Maybe if he tried very hard, he could persuade Susannah to—

He pushed open her door and his heart stopped. Susannah lay still in the white bed. In her arms she cradled the baby. Both of them were sleeping.

"Kiss her, Davy."

There were times when Darla was absolutely right. This was one of them. So David leaned forward and pressed his lips against Susannah's.

"When will you wake up and love me?" he murmured.

She blinked. Then she lifted her incredible lashes and smiled.

"Right now. I love you, David." She lifted her head for his kiss.

"See? Sleeping Beauty. I told you, Davy." Darla smiled at Susannah. "Davy needs to listen to me more often."

"Yes, I do." He smoothed a hand over Susannah's glistening hair, needing to touch her, to reassure himself that he wasn't dreaming.

"I'll hold Grace while you talk about the wedding," Darla said. She sat in a chair and held out her arms. "I'm ready."

David glanced at Susannah who nodded and smiled. He carefully lifted the tiny child away from her mother, feeling awkward and stupid and clumsy, but oh, so blessed.

"Hello, Grace," he whispered. "I'd really like to marry your mother. And I'd love to be your daddy. Do you think that would work for you?"

When he touched her cheek with his finger, the sleeping child lifted a hand and closed her tiny pink fingers around his. Tears welled in his eyes.

Oh, Lord. His heart overflowed with thanksgiving at the love that raced through him for this precious child. This Easter baby.

He handed Grace to Darla. Then he returned to Susannah's side.

"Please marry me, Susannah. Let me be a part of your life, and of Grace's. Be a part of mine and Darla's. Nobody could be a better mother to Grace than you," he added.

"I don't know if you're right about that, David," she whispered, wrapping her small hand in his. "But I'm going to give motherhood my very best effort."

"Darla was right you know," she said.

"She usually is." David loved the way her hand fit into his—he adored Susannah Wells. "But about what, specifically?"

"I was Sleeping Beauty. Well, maybe not the beauty part but I was sleeping, because until I met you, I didn't know what real love was. There are so many facets to love, but I know now that it all begins with God's love. That makes everyone worthy of love."

"Yes, it does. I believe God led you to Darla and me, that it was He who placed love in my heart for you. So—" David dragged out the word "—does that mean you are going to marry me, Susannah Wells?"

"Yes, please," she said with a smile.

"Finally." He wrapped his arms around her and kissed her the way he'd been longing to for weeks.

"But not right away." Susannah leaned back, her arms still circled around his neck.

"But—" He frowned when she placed a finger across his lips.

"I need time, David. Time to understand what it means to be a child of God. Time to understand what being your wife will mean. Time to understand how to be a mother to Grace and a sister to Darla."

"I'll be in a retirement home by then," he teased. But he loved her all the more for her wisdom. "Okay then. While you're figuring that out, I'm going to learn how to be a father. My first lesson will involve a trip to the toy store."

"I think you can start learning how to be a daddy right now, Davy." Darla held the baby toward him. "Grace needs her diaper changed."

Epilogue

Four months later, Susannah and David's wedding day dawned hot and glorious in the Arizona desert.

"I don't want all the frills and frou frou," she'd told David. "I've realized that it's what's in the heart that matters. Choose whatever you like for our wedding." Then she'd returned to walking colicky Grace across the pool deck.

David, being David, had gone beyond anything Susannah could have imagined and as she stood inside his house—their house—on her wedding day, waiting for the music to begin, she couldn't believe what he'd done for her.

For starters, David had asked Hornby to work magic on the backyard. Roses climbed and burst and bloomed everywhere, their fragrance filling the air. White chairs with bows dotted the lush green grass and nestled near a fountain that spilled water over desert rocks and stones. Fronting the fountain stood a white filigree bower decorated in more roses and Susannah's favorite—limelight hydrangeas.

"Aren't you glad I persuaded you to buy this suit?"

Connie whispered. "You look gorgeous, a perfectly dressed bride at her garden wedding."

"I only got into it because of all that swimming," Susannah whispered back. "I don't know what I'd have done without Darla to egg me on." But the truth was, the ivory shantung skirt and matching jacket looked stunning on her and she knew it.

She'd decided against a veil and chosen instead to weave a few bits of baby's breath through her upswept hair. Diamond hoops in her ears—David's wedding gift—were Susannah's only jewelry, aside from the beautiful yellow diamond solitaire on her ring finger.

"Are you ready, Susannah?" Connie asked.

"Yes." She was ready to marry her Prince Charming and begin the life God had given her.

Connie gave the signal and the soft melodious sounds of a wedding song filled the air. Darla went first, wearing her favorite red in a stylish sundress that showed her beauty. In her arms she carried Grace, decked out in a white frilly dress with red trim that displayed her chubby legs, and tiny feet clad in white ballet slippers. David's idea. He was going to spoil his daughter rotten, Susannah had realized.

Connie walked out of the house, her dress also red. And then all eyes turned to Susannah.

She was nervous at first. But then her gaze met David's.

This is the man God chose for me, she thought. *Because of God's grace I am worthy of love. I can give my heart to this wonderful man because I know that together we will share a future filled with joy and happiness. And love.*

She stepped confidently through the door and walked toward the man who'd taught her that love could grow to encompass everyone.

* * * * *

Dear Reader,

Hello there! Welcome back to Tucson and my LOVE FOR ALL SEASONS series. I hope you enjoyed Susannah and David's story. I love the beauty and variations in Arizona and it was again my privilege to set a story in this location. Susannah's story could be that of many women across North America—alone, in trouble and desperate to figure out the next move. She'd lost faith in everything and everyone except one old friend who had loved her when she needed it. David, too, fights a battle of loneliness. Loss and responsibility have bowed him with life's worries. It takes Susannah's special courage to open his eyes to possibilities. And Darla—well, what can you say about darling Darla? Darla faces bigger issues than many of us will ever know. But she keeps hanging on to her faith in our God who loves each of us dearly.

Thank you so much for your cards and letters. I love hearing from each of you and try hard to respond as quickly as I can. I treasure each kind word you've shared about my books. They touch me as I hope my books touch you. I hope you'll enjoy *A Family for Summer,* the next book in this series. Meantime, you can reach me at Box 639, Nipawin, SK Canada S0E 1E0, at www. loisricher.com or through Steeple Hill.

Until we meet again, my prayer is that you will experience all that Easter offers: joy overflowing, hope that never dies and peace, the kind of peace God meant us to celebrate at Easter.

Blessings,

Lois
Richer

QUESTIONS FOR DISCUSSION

1. Think of your church, your neighbourhood, your town. Is there anyone you know in a situation like Susannah's? Could you befriend them or offer some type of help?

2. Discuss Darla's simple faith and reasons why so many of us struggle with trust in God.

3. David felt the full weight of his responsibilities and didn't want to take on any more. Do you think this added to his issues with control? How can we guard against trying to keep ourselves "safe" in an unsafe world?

4. Susannah had made up her mind fairly early in the story that she was going to give her child up for adoption. Talk about ways we organize our worlds to accommodate preconceived ideas we hold about what is right and what is God's will.

5. Connie offered sanctuary, love and her faith to Susannah without asking a lot of questions. In your church and community, are there people like Connie, who simply offer help without judging? Could you be one of them? Why or why not?

6. Susannah challenged David when she felt he was wrong about Darla's needs. Discuss how we can learn when it is appropriate to question and when we need to keep our ideas to ourselves.

7. Susannah offers Darla solid, steady love, something Susannah never received from her own mother. Consider why giving love like this often frees the injured child inside.

8. Susannah's mother refused to see or talk to her daughter for many years—partly to ease her own guilt, but perhaps partly in a misguided effort to help Susannah move on. Was she wrong? Why or why not?

9. David made it his business to dig into Susannah's past in an effort to help her face the future. Do you think he was wrong? Would you go to the same extreme for a loved one?

10. David offered a plethora of options for adoption to Susannah. Are there misconceptions about adoption in your group? List the most common ones. Think about open adoptions where the birth mother has full access to the child.

11. Both Connie and Susannah benefited from rich childhoods made possible through the generosity of their foster parents. How do you feel about fostering? Would you consider it?

12. Psychologists (and Susannah) say that feelings of self-worth are the most important in developing a child's healthy inner concept. Clearly Connie and Susannah's foster parents did an excellent job of parenting and yet Susannah ran away from them. Discuss how a foster parent might deal with such apparent rejection.

13. Susannah finally realized that her lack of self-worth was something only she could end—that she had wallowed in those feelings because she wouldn't accept her value in God's eyes. How do we build our own feelings of self-worth without becoming conceited?

14. Compare Susannah's mistaken belief with some of your own deeply held tenets. Are they from God or are they your own personal take on a particular situation?

15. David embraced baby Grace as his own daughter. Indeed, he saw her as the answer to his prayer for a family. Could you do the same?

INSPIRATIONAL

Inspirational romances to warm your heart & soul.

Love Inspired®

TITLES AVAILABLE NEXT MONTH

Available April 26, 2011

AN UNLIKELY MATCH
Chatam House
Arlene James

MIRIAM'S HEART
Hannah's Daughters
Emma Miller

HOME TO STAY
Annie Jones

BIG SKY REUNION
Charlotte Carter

THE FOREST RANGER'S PROMISE
Leigh Bale

INSTANT DADDY
Carol Voss

REQUEST YOUR FREE BOOKS!

2 FREE INSPIRATIONAL NOVELS
PLUS 2
FREE
MYSTERY GIFTS

Love Inspired HISTORICAL

Save $1.00 when you purchase
2 or more Love Inspired® Historical books.

SAVE
$1.00
when you purchase 2 or more
Love Inspired® Historical books.

Coupon expires September 30, 2011. Redeemable at participating retail outlets in the U.S. and Canada only. Limit one coupon per customer.

52609783

5 65373 00076 2   (8100)0 11736

Canadian Retailers: Harlequin Enterprises Limited will pay the face value of this coupon plus 10.25¢ if submitted by customer for this specified product only. Any other use constitutes fraud. Coupon is nonassignable. Void if taxed, prohibited or restricted by law. Consumer must pay any government taxes. Void if copied. Nielsen Clearing House ("NCH") customers submit coupons and proof of sales to: Harlequin Enterprises Limited, P.O. Box 3000, Saint John, NB E2L 4L3, Canada. Non-NCH retailer: for reimbursement submit coupons and proof of sales directly to Harlequin Enterprises Limited, Retail Marketing Department, 225 Duncan Mill Rd., Don Mills, ON M3B 3K9, Canada. Limit one coupon per purchase. Valid in Canada only.

U.S. Retailers: Harlequin Enterprises Limited will pay the face value of this coupon plus 8¢ if submitted by customer for this specified product only. Any other use constitutes fraud. Coupon is nonassignable. Void if taxed, prohibited or restricted by law. Consumer must pay any government taxes. Void if copied. For reimbursement ,submit coupons and proof of sales directly to: Harlequin Enterprises Limited, P.O. Box 880478, El Paso, TX 88588-0478, U.S.A. Cash value 1/100 cents. Limit one coupon per purchase. Valid in the U.S. only.

LIHCOUPON1